A Candlelight Ecstasy Romance®

"WOULD HAVING AN AFFAIR WITH ME CREATE ANY SERIOUS PROBLEMS FOR YOU?" RALT ASKED.

Lee stared at him. "Why do you ask?"

"Oh," he said, shrugging, "it's time to make some changes in my personal life. And, all in all, I'd say we have a fair chance of making each other reasonably happy . . . for a while."

"Of course. And how is it possible for you to want to go to bed with me, when you know so little about me?" she asked sweetly.

"Believe me, honey, for two people to make love, it's not necessary for them to know each other's life histories."

"McLean's Rule, I'm sure." Lee nodded. "But I don't play by anyone's rules but my own. So take your offer and stuff it."

CANDLELIGHT ECSTASY CLASSIC ROMANCES

CANDLELIGHT ECSTASY ROMANCES®

A LOVER'S MYSTIQUE

Eleanor Woods

A CANDLELIGHT ECSTASY ROMANCE®

Published by
Dell Publishing Co., Inc.
1 Dag Hammarskjold Plaza
New York, New York 10017

Dell ® TM 681510, Dell Publishing Co., Inc.

Candlelight Ecstasy Romance®, 1,203,540, is a registered
trademark of Dell Publishing Co., Inc., New York, New York.

ISBN: 0-440-15032-9

Printed in the United States of America

May 1987

10 9 8 7 6 5 4 3 2 1

WFH

To Our Readers:

We have been delighted with your enthusiastic response to Candlelight Ecstasy Romances®, and we thank you for the interest you have shown in this exciting series.

In the upcoming months we will continue to present the distinctive sensuous love stories you have come to expect only from Ecstasy. We look forward to bringing you many more books from your favorite authors and also the very finest work from new authors of contemporary romantic fiction.

As always, we are striving to present the unique, absorbing love stories that you enjoy most—books that are more than ordinary romance. Your suggestions and comments are always welcome. Please write to us at the address below.

Sincerely,

The Editors
Candlelight Romances
1 Dag Hammarskjold Plaza
New York, New York 10017

A LOVER'S
MYSTIQUE

CHAPTER ONE

Leslie Elaine Cantrell, petite, green-eyed with dark curly hair, was affectionately known to family and friends as Lee. At the moment, she was a bundle of absolute fury as she ripped the letter from the portable typewriter, separated the original from the copy, then dropped back in her chair and began proofing it.

Her remarks were directed to a Mr. Arthur K. Lowe, V.P. Consumer Relations, in follow-up to a letter she'd written a little over a week before to Daniel F. Hunter, President. In the rather lengthy missive she was presently reading, Lee had "reinforced" her complaints more strongly than in her letter to Daniel F. Hunter, especially in view of the devastating experience she'd had earlier in the afternoon.

"Not only does my Model LA 36-42 Renmate washing machine give an impressive imitation of a crab crawl when in use, Mr. Lowe, it shimmies like a strip-tease artist.

"As of this afternoon, sir, my *wonderful* new washing machine has also consumed and/or chewed . . . you are reading correctly, Mr. Lowe, the words are consumed and/or chewed . . . one blouse, one each

9

of three pairs of socks, one bath towel, and three wash-cloths. These 'happenings' come without any advance notice. One may use the machine two, three times without mishap, then suddenly it becomes a monster.

"Please note the photographs I've enclosed as verification of my claim, accompanied by the properly notarized statement from Ms. Maria Bidding, who can attest to the legitimacy of my complaints. Note the huge holes in the material where they were pulled from beneath the agitator. Please be apprised of the fact that I'm firmly convinced a smaller version of 'Jaws' inhabits the piece of equipment placed on the market by your firm and purchased by me. Note also the position of the washing machine . . . *erupting* from the doorway of the laundry room as if being shot from a cannon. This is most disconcerting, Mr. Lowe. No one likes to own an appliance they think might attack them.

"None of the dealerships here in the New Orleans area have gone out of their way to try and help me with this supposedly 'unique' problem. Since the gentleman from whom I purchased the machine is no longer in business, I can only assume the other dealers are afraid of some sort of financial loss if they become involved.

"I would also like to point out, Mr. Lowe, that the amount of money owed me by Ban-Cor Manufacturing Company for personal items ruined continues to grow. The balance now comes to approximately ninety-four dollars."

Lee chewed at the eraser of the pencil she was idly twisting in one hand as she read the remaining typewritten lines. Finally satisfied that there was very little else she could do to improve it, she folded the letter and put it in the envelope.

A cup of coffee would taste good, she thought as she raised her arms over her head and edged into a bone-cracking stretch. She turned and started toward the kitchen just as the phone rang.

Lee walked faster to the wall phone in the kitchen. "Hello?" she said pleasantly enough despite the irritation brought on by the god-awful monster sitting behind louvered doors in the laundry room to her right. Actually it was nothing more than a long closetlike enclosure, but it served its purpose nicely.

"Ahh," a raspy voice sounded in her ear. "Is this the lady who buys kinky washing machines?"

"Certainly." Lee couldn't help but grin at the teasing quality of Cole Taggart's voice. She'd been working for him for approximately a year and a half. An instant rapport had sprung up between them, but Lee wasn't silly enough to think she really knew Cole. She doubted anyone ever would. "Do you have any clothes you'd like torn, mutilated, or devoured?"

"None that I can recall at the moment. However," Cole added silkily, "there are one or two people . . . Exactly how big is that damned machine?"

"Not that big, you bloodthirsty lug. What's on your mind?"

"Scratching around—looking for a way to make a buck, kid. Just trying to make a buck."

"I can't buy that." Lee laughed. "You're not starving. Not by a long shot." And he wasn't. His magazine, *Man's Viewpoint,* had been a solid success from its inception. Cole worked like a demon, and expected each of his employees to do the same. And even though Lee, at twenty-four, was the youngest member of the staff, she knew Cole expected her to contribute one hundred percent.

She'd worked for a newspaper directly after graduation, then when offered the chance to go to work for *Man's Viewpoint,* she'd jumped at the opportunity. A rapport had slowly evolved between Lee and Cole. Lee often thought she looked upon Cole as a father figure in her life. Certainly not an older brother because she was already blessed—or cursed—depending on one's particular point of view—with an older brother. Cole, on the other hand, would have been highly incensed had he known the surrogate role to which he'd been relegated in her life.

"I may be able to keep us afloat for a few months longer."

"Gee, I hope so, Cole," Lee commiserated with him in suspect sympathy. "I've got two weeks' vacation coming, and I'd sure hate to see us go under before I get a chance to enjoy it."

"Young people!" he exclaimed in a teasing tone, giving the impression his age of forty-one was as old as Moses. "I'm about to be evicted, and you're worried about your vacation time. Scandalous, simply scandalous! I've got an assignment for you, kid."

"I was afraid of that." Lee sighed. "What is it, an interview with the master whittler of Podunk Hollow?" Her last two assignments had really brought a howl of protest from Lee. She wanted a story with meat in it, something she could really get into. She wanted to "prove" herself.

"Ralt McLean."

"You know you owe me one, Cole. I've done everything at that magazine from running the sweeper to changing light bulbs. You gave Dan—" Her sudden spate of words dwindled to a mere whisper as she finally comprehended the name he'd spoken. "Did you say Ralt McLean? 'The' Ralt McLean? The same one who has been known to smash cameras and tear up note pads belonging to photographers and reporters?"

"Is there more than one?" Cole chuckled.

"I hope not! From what I've heard about the devilish man, he's mean enough for three. May I ask why you've chosen him?"

"He's news . . . always. Plus no other publication has gotten near him for years. Many have tried, but none has succeeded."

"So you decide to toss this impossible task my way, and not bother your other, more experienced staff members. Correct?" she asked curtly. One day she would show them, she thought grimly, immediately forgetting the journalistic awards she'd been garnering since her college days when she was working to help pay her way through school. She was good. Damned good. But she seemed always to be the youngest one on the ladder, the least experienced, and her present position was no exception. She was the youngest at *Man's Viewpoint,* and she'd been the last reporter to be hired. That annoyed hell out of her. It was a foregone conclusion she would get the leftovers, reasoning that it would keep her occupied till something more "suit-

13

able" for her came along. Lee was finding it more and more difficult these days to control her disappointment.

"Why, Leslie Elaine." Cole infuriated her by calling her by her full given name. "Are you afraid you can't handle it—or him? He's only a man, honey. Haven't you always told me that you're just as good as any man working for me?"

"Yes," she snapped.

"Well then, dear girl, here's your chance to prove it."

"How long do I have on this great, miserable failure?"

"Approximately two and a half months."

"That's all?" she cried in dismay. Damn! It would take her that long just to find out where that miserable McLean was keeping himself. Everybody knew he was an expert at keeping a low profile.

"What do you want, an entire year?" Cole railed at her.

"It would help, you obnoxious twit. You know perfectly well that I have to find this damned Ralt McLean first. Do you have any suggestions just where I should begin? From where I stand, I might as well be the prime target in an almighty snipe hunt."

"Snipe hunts have been Southern tradition for no telling how long. Could be indulged in in other parts of the country, but I can't be sure of that. Ever been on a snipe hunt, Lee?" Cole chuckled.

Her silence brought a further guffaw of amusement from her "gentle and compassionate" employer. "I can see that you have. Well," he exhaled noisily into the mouthpiece, a gesture he knew would further annoy her, "do the best you can. If you find the going too rough, I can always send Dan. Better yet, Isobel might want a crack at the mighty Ralt. It's said he's something of a killer with women."

"Gee, I can hardly wait to cast myself into his loving arms and swoon upon his chest."

"God, that was bad."

"Not any worse than the lousy blackmail attempt you just tried," she quipped. "Send Dan or Isobel, indeed. Why the hell don't you send them to start with?"

"Because I've learned one thing about you, Leslie Elaine, darling. You are without a doubt the most stubborn female on God's green earth. As such," he went on in his rusty voice, "I'm willing to put my money on you. If anyone can run Ralt McLean to ground, it's you. Besides that, you're hungry for a chance. Nothing motivates like necessity."

"How is it possible for a human being to be so two-faced? First you imply you aren't sure I can do the job, then you do an about-face and throw a few words of praise my way and expect me to roll over like a performing seal, then you insult me again."

"I'm crushed . . . truly crushed. I offer you my trust and support and you repay me by accusing me of being deceitful."

"You'll recover," she said sourly. "In the meantime, may I assume you'll have something for me in the way of leads? Or am I to go out cold turkey and canvass the streets of New Orleans, Houston, and Dallas for information on Ralt McLean?"

15

"Well . . ." Cole drawled maddeningly, "if you really insist." At the muffled exclamation in his ear, he grinned—enormously pleased. She'd do a hell of a fine job and he knew it. "Come by in the morning and we'll go over all that we have."

After she finished talking with Cole, Lee walked back into the living room, still chafing from his teasing, but so tickled with the assignment she could hardly stand it.

Lee walked over to the front door and double-checked the lock. As she came back across the room, she turned off the two lamps bathing the room in their glow, then continued on to her bedroom.

She glanced at the small clock on her bedside table and saw it was only ten thirty. Not late, but for some reason she was tired. Her gaze caught sight of the edge of an envelope partially hidden by the mystery she'd been trying to read for a month.

Lee reached for the envelope, raised the flap, and removed the single sheet of stationery and the two tickets. A soft tremulous smile touched her lips as she reread the brief letter.

Lance Porter. Mrs. Lance Porter. That name used to sound perfect to her, Lee told herself. Lance had been her idol through high school and on into college. They'd married when she was a junior and he a senior.

She'd been a cheerleader and he'd been the captain of the football team—they'd been the perfect couple—until they both realized that making a marriage work was far more complicated than playing football and attending cheerleading clinics. Neither of them had sense enough to realize that the love they'd thought

16

they felt for each other was nothing more than a friendship with a healthy sex drive thrown in to cloud the issues.

The divorce had been friendly. Why not? Lee thought on a sad but relieved note. She didn't hate Lance, nor he, her. What she did hate was that they'd ruined a beautiful friendship by getting married. They'd lost something sweet, something she knew could never be recaptured. She missed the good times. There was still a great deal of resentment in her because of the divorce. Her experience with Lance had soured her on marriage. How could two people ever be sure?

She glanced down at the tickets in her hand. Lance and the California Wingers would meet the New Orleans Flames in the superdome in a week. He was the number one quarterback for the Wingers. He was also in medical school, and planned to specialize in sports medicine. As was his habit since their divorce, Lance had sent her tickets to the game each time they played in New Orleans.

Sometimes Lee and Harry Osgood, an old friend, used the tickets, sometimes she gave them away. Occasionally Lance would call her when he was on the road, and he always telephoned her when he was in town. The conversations were light and lively enough, yet Lee could feel the strain. The magic was gone, but the tie wasn't broken, damn it! No longer were they friends, neither were they enemies, they had become polite strangers, and it hurt like hell. They seemed incapable of carrying on a conversation with each other

17

without some innocently spoken word reminding them of another place and time.

Lee wondered when they would stop trying to make the effort. They'd been divorced over a year, she thought sadly as tears filled her eyes. A rush of frustration swept over her as she silently railed against the fates that had stirred their caldron of confusion and created an illusion that had culminated in marriage. A marriage that had left two decent people feeling as if they'd been run over by a freight train. They'd each lost a good friend, and they were still bereft, still smarting.

Again she stared at the two tickets in her hand. After several thoughtful moments, she tore them in half, then walked over and dropped them and the letter into the trash basket.

I'm sorry, Lance, she thought quietly, tears gently easing their way down her cheeks, but we have to let it die.

"Hmm." Lee exhaled generously the next morning, cocking her head at first one angle and then another as she stared at a five-by-seven photo of a very big man. Ralt McLean was tall. Wide. His shoulders appeared broad and strong, and he looked mean.

It was obvious from the look on his face that, as usual, he hadn't been pleased to have his picture taken. He was frowning, every feature tensed and drawn together in a disapproving mask. Lee saw an iron chin with a perfect cleft in it. She also saw penetrating eyes that made her shiver with their lack of warmth. From what she could make out, and from the few times she'd seen him on the television news, it looked as if Ralt McLean had black hair.

She directed her green eyes toward her boss, his thick, dark hair with the silver wings at the temples slightly mussed from his unconscious habit of raking his hand through it when something was bothering him. Cole Taggart was of medium to tall height, with a husky build. His hazel eyes seemed never to miss a thing, and Lee knew he had a very practiced eye for the ladies.

At the moment, Cole was sitting with his feet propped up on one corner of the long, polished table, quietly sipping his coffee and watching Lee. "What have I done to you that would cause you to cast this death wish on me?" They were in what was laughingly referred to as the "conference room" by members of the magazine staff. Actually it was an area that served as general catchall for extra files to a thirty-two-pot coffee maker that stayed plugged in from seven in the morning till eight or nine at night.

"I beg your pardon?" Cole spoke innocently.

"This." She held up the photo and waved it. "This isn't a man. This is a Sherman tank masquerading as a human being. Just looking at him gives me the willies."

A thoughtful expression slitted across Cole's face as he studied the likeness of Ralt McLean. "You're right, of course. You're entirely too young to take on such a person. The man's a tyrant, his temper unbelievable. Why, it's been said that McLean can leave mere mortals quivering with fright from a single look. Vic-

19

tims of his verbal attacks suffer from a case of nerves for days afterward."

"I'm *not* too young, Mr. Taggart." Lee glared at him. "And you can stop with your cute innuendos. I've accepted the assignment. What else do you want . . . my signature, sealing the bargain, written in blood?"

"Gee. Would you?"

Lee retaliated by sticking out her tongue at him, then turned her attention back to the voluminous file before her and studied it for several minutes. "I would like to know," she muttered finally in a voice as if alone, "what there is about this individual that drives him to be such an ass. Rumor has it, he's conceited as the very devil."

"Money." Cole shrugged. "He's fantastically successful, honey. Everything he touches turns to gold. He's had it all, the hard work, the women, and the hype that goes along with it. All he's asking is to be left alone. There's some old rumor about an unpleasant incident regarding a reporter and McLean's second wife's death."

She regarded him skeptically. "Naturally, you don't know any of the details."

"Maybe . . . maybe not. I prefer you find out for yourself."

"Why do you sound as if you approve of his attitude toward you and your peers?"

"Because in a way I suppose I do."

"Then why on earth am I about to brave the wilds of his beastly temper for a lousy story?" Lee demanded.

"Because he's a damned newsworthy subject, and I run a very successful magazine. That happens to take precedence over my approval of his attitude. I can't think of a single reporter who wouldn't give their eyeteeth to get at Ralt McLean. Over the years he's created a love-hate relationship with the media that's become something of a mystique. In fact," he grinned, "that might not be a bad title for your piece: 'The Mystique of Ralt McLean.' "

Lee lifted one shoulder dismissively. "I'll think about it." Actually it did sound good, she told herself, but she'd be damned if she would admit it. Perhaps later, when she'd actually met McLean, and had gotten some insight into the man and his moods. Until then, every thought, idea and word would be pure Lee Cantrell.

"You said last night that I had approximately two and a half months. That deadline still stand?" she asked.

"More or less." Cole nodded. "By the way, rumor has it that McLean's been seeing a woman named Althea Graham for a number of weeks. She's from an old Houston family—an old 'broke' Houston family."

"Ahhh." Lee nodded knowingly. "Usual story, eh? I'm surprised Ms. Graham isn't more original. 'Trying to get sweet ol' Ralt to the altar, is she?"

Cole lifted his hands in a gesture of vagueness. "I haven't the faintest idea."

"Now why can't I believe you?" Lee frowned. "I wouldn't be at all surprised if you made up that little tidbit of information." She pushed back her chair and got to her feet. "May I take this home with me?" She indicated the thick folder she'd picked up and was holding in her arms.

"Certainly." Cole smiled cheekily. "Never let it be said that the inestimable editor in chief of such a distinguished magazine as *Man's Viewpoint* ever—for one tiny second—stood in the way of a woman reporter realizing her full potential.

Lee stared at him chagrined. "Okay," she finally said, "so I've been a bit on edge. You're a paragon of fairness. You're a fantastic person to work for." She lifted her hands, palms up. "What more can I say?"

"Oh I'm sure there's much more." He grinned. "I don't mind in the least waiting for something else to come to mind."

"Your ego's been stroked enough," Lee remarked as she turned and walked across the room. She paused. "You do know this will mean any number of short hops between here and Houston, don't you?"

"We'll survive."

That night, after a busy afternoon of research, coffee with her best friend and neighbor Maria Bidding, then a light supper of soup and salad, Lee finally settled down in bed, the file on Ralt McLean strewn over the patchwork coverlet.

The man was either depicted as saint or sinner. The press couldn't seem to make up its mind. He was head of a huge conglomerate, and the firm hand he exercised in the running of his vast empire was detailed in a number of articles.

Lee's lips pursed slightly when she read accounts of two marriages. The first one—lasting two years—ended in divorce. His second marriage, while seeming happy enough from the two or three articles she read and several photos of the smiling couple, had ended tragically. He'd married the daughter of the man who had given him his start, and she had been kidnapped. The ransom was paid but Mrs. McLean had been found dead five days later. Other women came and went in the written account of Ralt McLean's activities, but no other serious relationships were mentioned.

Money. Tragedy.

Those two words kept running through Lee's mind as she continued reading. She was also struck by the uncomfortable idea that she had somehow assumed the unflattering role of a peeping Tom, standing at the window of Ralt McLean's mind and staring into the myriad thoughts, emotions, faults, and saving graces of the man. She'd never felt that way before . . . why now?

From the account of his endowing an orphanage in Arizona for the care of Indian children, she could only assume there was some hidden thread of kindness running through him. There were also other charities to which he contributed: a large monetary gift to a retirement home; a new roof, new books, and desks for a country school in a west Texas community. The list went on. But was it really kindness, Lee wondered?

She read till the hands of the clock slipped well past midnight. It was because the material was interesting, she told herself, not wanting to acknowledge that Ralt McLean had begun to fill her mind and wasn't as easily forgotten as her usual stories.

When she could no longer keep her eyes open, Lee

eased it to the floor beside the bed, turned off the lamp, then slipped down in bed and pulled the sheet up to her shoulders.

"I know it's old Mossy Back, boss," Raz Cutlitt continued his lengthy monologue. Raz had worked for Ralt for years, and was as avid a sportsman as his boss. "Daniel's been watching that particular watering hole for weeks now. Never could get a good look at him till day before yesterday. Says he's big, Ralt, damned big. Says he looks mean and cunning too."

"The Nilgai are born cunning, Raz," Ralt McLean remarked with wry amusement. He leaned back in his large chair and propped his booted feet on the corner of an ornately carved antique desk, his lids narrowed as he considered his hectic schedule. "What about you and me flying down toward Raymondville one day this week? Call and see about accommodations for one night at Finn's Lodge. If we're lucky, maybe we'll get a shot at this monster you assure me is there."

"You sure you can get loose?"

"Hell yes, I'm sure. What's wrong. Afraid your precious Nilgai won't be there after all?"

"He's there all right," Raz hastily assured him, excitement edging his voice. "I saw him with my own eyes six months ago. He's a trophy shot, Ralt. Must weigh at least seven hundred pounds."

"Good. Let's hope one of us can bag him. If you don't hear from me before then, I'll pick you up at the ranch on Tuesday morning . . . early. Oh, and Raz—"

"Yeah, Boss?"

"Keep quiet about where we'll be going, and remind Finn that I don't want a damned retinue of reporters following me through the brush."

"Hell, boss," Raz remarked, clearly affronted. "You don't have to remind me of something like that. I've been playing bodyguard—of a sort—for nigh on sixteen years now."

"Just being careful, Raz," Ralt smoothed the older man's ruffled feathers. "By the way, how's that bunch of new heifers doing?"

"Great. Another day and they'll be ready to move over to the north pasture. Doc was out yesterday and gave them a clean bill of health. Said you'd bought yourself some fine ones."

"Anything else going on?"

"We lost five head of cattle two nights ago. Oh, that Josh Emmett called here the other day. Said he'd called you several times at the office and thought he might catch you here."

"He finally got me. He wants me to head up a commission to try to come up with some quick and innovative ideas that would help combat the illegal alien problem. That includes trying to get the ranchers in the south and southwestern part of the state to join forces in trying to help halt the influx from Mexico."

"Sounds noble and all that crap, Boss, but it's dangerous as hell. Did you point out to the good senator what happened to Sam Hayman last year when he tried to help out with a similar project? Did you tell him that we lost a barn with eight fine horses in it in retaliation for your work with Sam? And did you also inform him how we go over and help Sam's widow now—and a fairly young widow at that—take care of the ranch chores? Of Sam's two children growing up without their father?"

"You're getting old, Raz," Ralt said gruffly. "I most certainly am aware of all the things you've so graciously pointed out to me, my friend. But the problem still exists. Illegal entry to this country across the Mexican border truly comes under the heading of incredible. Sad thing about it, a good number of the poor stiffs are being thrown into work camps. Then there's always the 'kind gringo' who takes their money, gets them across the river . . . most of the time . . . then packs them like sardines in enclosed trucks to transport them to God knows where. You know as well as I do there's no telling how many of them die during that ordeal."

"Which should let you know that you don't want to get involved with the kind of people who traffic in illegal aliens. Damn, Ralt, it's dangerous as hell. So tell me," he asked cautiously. "What was your answer to Emmett?"

"I said I'd head up the committee."

"You're a damned fool!"

"An opinion which I'm sure is shared by a number of people, Raz," Ralt agreed mockingly. "It wouldn't hurt to take on some extra hands for a few months."

"I'll take care of it first thing in the morning."

"By the way, don't try to do anything about the rustling. When I get there, we'll work on the problem then."

"Will do."

"Good. Okay." Ralt exhaled noisily. "See you on

Tuesday, Raz. I'll be in and out of the state till then, so if you need me, get in touch with Miriam and have her find me."

After the conversation was over, Ralt sat back with his large hands locked behind his head, his gaze moving disinterestedly from one object in the spacious office to another.

Finally he ran a callused palm over his face, smothering a huge yawn. What the hell was the matter with him? But he knew the answer even before he asked the question. He was tired.

Maybe Raz's short hunting trip was what he needed, Ralt thought as he lowered his feet to the floor and sat forward. He began releasing the buttons of the white shirt he'd been wearing since six o'clock that morning. If he was to make it for dinner at Althea Graham's house by eight o'clock, he'd have to hurry. It was already seven twenty-five.

Ralt rose to his massive height, his large size and the spaciousness of the room complementing each other. According to the note pinned to his blanket when he was found as an abandoned infant in a bus station thirty-eight years ago, he was of Scottish, Irish, and Apache heritage. At that precise moment he looked more like his Apache ancestors than any of the others. A hard-bitten smile tore at Ralt's lips as he considered the mixture of his lineage. Having descended from three races known for their stubbornness, he decided with amusement, must account for the media comparing him to a jackass of the Missouri variety.

He deserted the office through a door to the left of

his desk, and entered a small suite with an adjoining bath that was almost a must for his busy life-style. He quickly fixed himself a Scotch and water from a bar tucked unobtrusively in one corner and took a long sip.

Though the name of Ralt McLean meant megabucks and power to those in the corporate vein, the man to whom the name belonged was totally unaffected by the wealth he'd amassed or the deference accorded him because of that wealth. Oh, he enjoyed it, he silently acknowledged as he set the glass down, undressed, then headed for the shower. He enjoyed it to the hilt. Yet at the same time, he often found himself looking with amusement upon the position of respect he'd carved for himself, often wondering how "respectable" he'd be if he were to suddenly become bankrupt.

Would his so-called friends still toady to him if he were flat broke? he mused a brief time later as he strolled through the sitting room to the closet, his powerful bronzed body naked except for a towel hanging over one broad shoulder.

Hell no, he thought grimly, feeling a certain loathing for the individuals who fawned over him, who would practically kill to get in his good graces. He only had three really good friends. His foreman Raz, Douglas Nelson, his father-in-law, and Steve Crandle, a neighboring rancher. His mouth pursed in a rueful twist. He wasn't so bad off after all. Three friends meant a hell of a lot.

He turned from pulling on a pair of dark pants and

28

shrugging into a clean white shirt, letting his gaze touch on the cozy niche he'd had created for himself.

Two paintings—both western scenes by Remington, showed Ralt's love for the West. Next his eyes sought the soothing quality of the handwoven Indian blanket in black, red, and orange thrown over one end of an extra-long sleep sofa which was a comfortable bed, as Ralt had learned many times in the past. An accumulation of chairs, tables, lamps, and several scattered pots of greenery had been brought together to create a casual but relaxed setting. The decorator had succeeded. The room offered Ralt—who spent a great deal of his time in his office, the hub of his empire—a touch of comfort away from the different apartments in various cities he called home. A walk-in closet filled with a complete wardrobe from boots to Stetsons completed the setting.

Who was he kidding? he mused mockingly. Home to him would never be anywhere but the sprawling ranch in the hill country, next to the Guadalupe River.

He inhaled deeply, unable to place a finger on the sense of unrest assailing him.

Tired . . . Bored?

That last word suddenly shot through his mind like a steel-tipped arrow. He was tired, yes. But he was also one hundred and ninety-nine percent bored. His life had become a series of corporate battles, business trips, boring social events . . . and women. No woman in particular. He would see one for a few weeks, then move on to another.

Where, he asked himself, was the satisfaction that should have come with the wealth he'd amassed? Why was there still a certain emptiness inside him? He certainly wasn't the nameless infant now.

But no matter how hard he tried, Ralt felt utterly and completely alone. He wondered what it would be like to have a wife and children waiting at home for him at the end of each day.

Don't be ridiculous, his saner half chided him. *Marriage and children can never be for you . . .*

He rubbed at a scar on his left shoulder, an old wound from Nam. He felt exactly as he used to when he was sitting in some foxhole with a foot or two of water, guns thundering around him, and the screams and moans of human beings that brought the glazed look in his cold, desolate eyes.

Well, he told himself, he was no longer fighting for his life, but happiness was still as damned elusive as finding that one woman there was supposed to be for every man in the world. *Be realistic,* he told himself. Boredom was the crux of the problem, but he couldn't displace the ridiculous notion that he was lonely as well.

How was that possible? He was a millionaire. People jumped at the chance to do his slightest bidding. He could have a continuous entourage if he chose. At times it was embarrassing at how preferentially he was treated. He thought of Althea, waiting for him to join her. But the picture of the tall, statuesque blonde failed to raise his body temperature one teeny bit. She left him cold as ice. He slowly shook his head, realizing he was in worse shape than he'd realized. What female did he know that was capable of jerking him out of the black mood he was in? Ralt wondered. But he couldn't think of a single one.

His expression became grim as he contemplated the scene that would end the evening, a scene that was bound to be embarrassing, but was inevitable.

Althea had definite plans of becoming the third Mrs. Ralt McLean. That was a very bad mistake on her part, Ralt mused. He'd told her repeatedly that he would never remarry. Two loveless marriages had been enough for him. Unfortunately, Althea hadn't listened. The Grahams needed money, and they weren't in the least averse to their daughter marrying to ensure that the family coffers be replenished.

No sir, Ralt thought without a great deal of feeling, Althea wouldn't take too kindly to being booted out of his life. But when a man was as bored and jaded as he'd become . . . He gazed into space. Exit the very lovely Althea Graham, enter . . . ?

CHAPTER TWO

Lee stared disbelieving at the panel of gauges in the rental car. What the devil was wrong? From where the needle was resting it looked as if there were still half a tank of gas left. The temperature was well within normal limits, so . . .

She turned the key again, heard the same noise an engine makes when it's trying to start, but that was all. It didn't start, and she was getting angry.

Through the limbs of the scrub oak in front of her, she could see the colorful dots that were the hot-air balloons growing smaller and smaller. Pictures of the balloonists and a short story of their experiences, she had decided earlier in the comfortable confines of her motel room, would please her boss and would also put her in the area where she'd heard Ralt McLean was sure to be found.

"Are you positive he's down there?" she'd asked Maria.

"Well, I wouldn't put my head on a block and tell you to chop it off if you don't find him, you idiot." The short, pert blonde grinned. "But according to my source, your pigeon is supposed to be in or around

Raymondville toward the middle of the week. One of the guys at my office has a brother who works at a hunting lodge down there. Seems Ralt McLean made a reservation." Maria's news had Lee floating on cloud nine.

Unfortunately, her cloud nine had turned to mud, she was thinking as she pulled a tiny lever, then got out and raised the hood and peered underneath.

"Amazing! Simply amazing." There were enough nuts and bolts and belts and weird-looking things all bunched up together to build a flaming jet engine! The only other time she'd seen under the hood of a car had been when her brother Ian had taken her shopping for her small compact. She felt almost sacrilegious for not knowing more about what she was now staring at so intently.

With a tentative hand, she reached out and tapped the knuckles against a huge round thing that contributed God only knew what to the workings of the engine. That wasn't so bad, she congratulated herself. At any rate, it always worked in the movies, didn't it? Why not for her. Filled with newfound confidence, she moved on to more complicated and greater achievements—she wiggled a few hoses, and even got brave enough to pull loose several wires, then plug them back in. Confident that she'd reconnected whatever it was that had somehow become disconnected, she got back into the car, turned on the key . . . and got the same damned thing she'd been getting for almost thirty minutes!

"Damnation!" she swore with all her might, gritting her teeth and longing for something to hit. Lee's hands

33

dropped into her lap, palms up. Her head flopped against the seat as she stared toward the heavens. "Why me?" she asked in a comically repressed voice. "What have I ever done to deserve the likes of the last few miserable days of my life?"

As she talked to herself, she got out of the car, jammed her purse under one arm, slammed the door, then began to walk along the barely discernible track through the brush, thankful she'd worn jeans and track shoes. "Frankly," she continued to speak, waving her hands for emphasis, "I don't give a damn whether or not I ever find Mr. McLean. To put it in a nutshell, I'm already sick of the man, his name, and the sneaky way he creeps around. If he wants to be a hermit, then let him. All I want to do is get out of this godforsaken wilderness and back to civilization."

She couldn't be more than a mile or two from the hunting lodge where the balloonists were to lift off. Once off the main road, she'd only made one or two turns into the brush before coming up on the large clearing and the dozen or so people. When they learned she was a reporter for a major magazine, they were eager to answer all and any questions. They even offered to take her up with them. Lee refused, feeling a little disappointed not to have found Ralt McLean in the group. On the other hand, expecting to find a man such as McLean with balloonists was stretching it a bit thin. Hunting was more likely to be his reason for being in the area. Yet the staff at the lodge had acted as though they'd never heard of Ralt McLean. She thought of trying to bribe one of them, but when she considered the amount of McLean's tips in comparison to the amount she would have to bribe with, she was embarrassed at her own thoughts.

Suddenly Lee came to a fork in the trail that was growing more difficult to follow by the second. She stopped, utter confusion lining her face. Which trail had she come in on? She rubbed her hands together nervously as she tried to remember some identifying tree or object, but everything looked the same. Flat. Drab. Scrub oaks, mesquite, even a few cedars, and the ever-present brush greeted her eyes in every direction. And even though it was the middle of November, it was still warm. The pink shirt she was wearing was plastered to her back, and she could feel the rivulets of perspiration running down between her breasts.

Finally, Lee started off to the right. It might be wrong, she told herself, but it sure beat the hell out of standing around doing nothing.

As she walked, she was steadily cursing Ralt McLean, damning him for all the trouble he'd caused her. For at least the last four days, she'd had no luck at all in running to ground the elusive McLean. Frankly, she was beginning to think the man was a damned phantom, and that occasionally the individual who portrayed him was brought out, a few snapshots taken of him, and he was immediately trundled back to obscurity.

Her mind went into overdrive. Perhaps the man was dead, and the people within his organization were afraid to let it be known for fear of causing Anmac's stock to take a tumble, thus throwing the entire conglomerate into a corporate tailspin.

Could such a thing be possible? Lee began to warm

35

to the idea. Then she began to rehearse the speech she could give Cole as she tried to convince him to her way of thinking.

The sound of loud voices brought her to an abrupt halt.

Her mind was into an absolute break dance of panic. Here she was, in the middle of nowhere with no means of defending herself—a prime target for any pervert that happened to come her way!

She looked about wildly. Should she try to make a run for it?

Run where? a tiny voice asked incredulously. You shouldn't be here in the first place. Why didn't you wait till that damned Ralt McLean was in Houston or New Orleans or some other civilized place? Why didn't you simply camp out on his doorstep? But no, not you, the voice jeered. You had to do it the hard way. Show the world . . . and your boss that you were as good as the other boys. Well, fellow, let's see you get yourself out of this little scrap.

Lee forced herself to place one foot ahead of the other, once, twice and so on till she'd walked at least ten slow paces, when she heard the crackling noise in the brush behind her.

She was so frightened she didn't dare turn her head for fear of what she would see, yet she was terrified that if she stayed still she'd surely be ripped to pieces by some wild beast.

The voices in front of her were louder now, yet she could barely hear them over the god-awful pounding of her heart. She happened to glance down at the front of her shirt, and saw it quivering with the vibrations.

Get hold of yourself, she lashed out in a silent attempt to control her very fertile imagination. *First you're frightened because you're alone, now you're cowering like some idiot because you hear voices. What's it to be?*

Without thinking, she opened her mouth. "Help!" The sound of her voice resembled a rusty gate swinging open.

Lee took a deep breath and tried again, during the same time that she was rushing headlong through the brush toward the only other human sounds in the vast nothingness she found herself in. "Help! Can anybody hear me?" she cried out again loud enough to wake the dead. "Is anybody out there?" She stumbled into a small clearing just as the words erupted from her lips.

"There sure as hell is," an angry giant in faded jeans, a bright orange vest and cap returned in a sarcastic retort as he whipped around to face her. Dark glasses shielded his eyes, and the brim of the cap was pulled low over his face. Remaining perfectly still, Lee chewed nervously at one corner of her bottom lip, eyeing the gun he was holding. There was something vaguely familiar about the absolutely furious individual facing her. But what? Was she supposed to know this character? Another man, similarly dressed, had appeared as well at her untimely intrusion and was now staring at her as if not quite believing his eyes. He also carried a gun.

Lee fidgeted nervously beneath the twin glares, not sure but what she wouldn't have been better off at the mercy of whatever monster there had been lurking in the brush behind her.

37

She raised one hand a few tentative inches, then let it drop. "H-hi," she managed to get past the huge knot of fear lodged in her throat and threatening to choke her dead on the spot. "My . . . My c-car won't start." The tall one was giving off the most unbelievable vibes of anger she'd ever encountered. Even without being able to see his eyes, Lee knew they would be as frigid as the Arctic.

"Hear that, Raz?" the tall, broad-shouldered man said in a deep, husky voice that sent plain unadulterated fear racing up and down Lee's spine, his concealed gaze never leaving her face. "Her car won't start."

Raz nodded. Actually he felt sorry for the girl, but he wasn't about to say so. Ralt was mad as hell, and once that happened, there was no stopping him. "Maybe I could have a look at her car, Boss. I'm pretty good at fixing things."

"She appears in the middle of the forest and announces that she has car trouble. What do we look like, your neighborhood mechanics?" Ralt took a menacing step toward Lee. "Car trouble! Do you realize that you spooked a trophy shot?" As he spoke, his voice increased in volume till it resembled the roar of a steam engine. "We were minding our own business, enjoying a few hours of relaxation, when we're interrupted by a damned idiot woman, whining about her car." He pinned Lee with a totally disgusted glare for a few seconds, then whipped around and began gathering up some strange-looking items and throwing them into a camouflaged case.

Idiot woman indeed. Just who the hell did he think he was anyway? Lee fumed. "I did say I'm sorry."

"She's sorry." Ralt snorted derisively, throwing Raz a knowing look. "How generous. Fifty dollars says she's a reporter," he muttered grimly.

"You're on," the older man grinned. What the hell. If she was a reporter, then she deserved to be dressed down. Ralt went to a great deal of trouble and expense to enjoy a few hours hunting. Either way, Raz knew he'd wind up fixing her car for her.

"Well?" Ralt turned his dark head toward Lee, who was becoming angrier by the minute. "Which one of them do you work for? And please," he sneered as he removed the dark glasses, "don't add insult to injury by telling me that it's one of the supermarket slime rags."

Lee stared incredulously! He had blue eyes . . . as blue as a robin's egg, and she'd found him. Cole would never believe her. Her own eyes almost bulged from her head as she stared and stared and stared. It was Ralt McLean in the flesh. All six feet five inches of him. At least that was what she'd read somewhere . . . that he was six feet, five inches tall. He was also devastating. His chin was awesome. Also, she thought fleetingly, he was huge, and mean-looking, and madder than hell at her. How was she ever going to get a story from the blasted man now? "I was beginning to think you didn't exist," she blurted out, then immediately wanted to cut out her tongue.

Ralt refused to be swayed by her honest outburst, though he did have to admit she was by far the most attractive reporter he'd encountered. He'd never seen jeans look any nicer on a woman, even though she was small for his taste. He liked his women tall. She was also the youngest. He scowled. "You are a reporter, aren't you?"

"I'm employed by a very reputable publication, Mr. McLean," she informed him levelly. "And even though I've quite obviously ruined your day, I find your behavior inexcusable." Even Cole wouldn't expect her to let the man treat her like dirt.

Ralt turned to Raz, his expression of suspect politeness causing the foreman to duck his head and rub at his chin. "She finds my behavior inexcusable, Raz. Did you hear that?"

"Sure did, Boss. Sure did." Raz nodded, though privately he was beginning to wish Ralt would simmer down a little. Hell, the girl didn't look to be no more than nineteen or twenty. More than that, she really did look scared. She was a pretty little thing too.

"Miss . . . whatever your name is, I don't give a flaming damn what your opinion is of me. Understand? I came down here for a few hours of pleasure. The minute I set my sights on old Mossy Back, you come flying out of the bush, screaming like some damned banshee. Mossy Back is at least ten miles from here at this very moment, and I'm stuck with you. Come to think of," he began deliberately, his gaze suggestive as it slowly covered each delectable inch of her diminutive shape, "I might just decide to hang you on my wall."

"Need I point out that I didn't deliberately get lost?" Lee snapped, ignoring the remark. Though for all her bravado, there was a definite tremor in her voice. Surely the ill-tempered brute was only kidding? Worse than that, what on earth had possessed her to use his name? She'd hoped to be able to get through the unpleasant encounter without ever actually admitting she recognized him. That way, she reasoned, when she did corner him for an interview in more conducive surroundings, there could at least be the element of surprise—feigned though it would be—from her. Now, however, she'd blown that not-so-original idea. There was no way in hell Ralt McLean was going to grant her an interview.

Apparently he was an avid hunter . . . in fact she was certain he was, from the research she'd done on him. With her misfortune of having scared off a trophy shot, she was positive she would be number one on his personal hate list.

After considering her for several more disturbing seconds, Ralt waved a large hand at Raz. "Want to pay up now or later?"

"Later." Raz chuckled. "Right now, I think we'd better take a look at Miss . . . er." He looked questioningly at Lee.

"Cantrell," she said defeatedly, "Leslie Cantrell."

"And just what brings a Leslie Cantrell to this part of Texas on this particular afternoon?" Ralt snapped.

For a brief moment Lee considered trying to get by with some totally fictitious story but she decided on the truth—partially. "I was doing a story on the balloonists."

"And who did you say you worked for?" Ralt asked, his hands thrust into the back pockets of his jeans. His feet were spread wide apart, and Lee felt as she were facing the inquisitioner.

She hesitated, loath to reveal the name of the magazine. "I really can't see that it's any of your business, Mr. McLean. All I'm asking of you or," she nodded toward Raz, "this gentleman, is to take a look at my car and see if you can help me."

"Don't try to make a deal, honey, when you don't have anything to deal with. That's stupid. Who do you work for?" Ralt repeated in a voice so quiet, a hush seemed to fall over them.

"Man's Viewpoint," she replied with ill grace.

"You were covering the assent of five balloonists in the Rio Grande Valley for a magazine based in New Orleans?" Ralt asked disbelievingly.

Lee had the grace to blush at the disparaging overtones in his voice. She dropped her gaze, wanting nothing more than to get in her car and get the hell away from Ralt McLean. Frankly, she hoped she never saw the man again. In less time than she cared to think about, he'd become the bane of her existence.

"Yes."

"With the hopes that the story of car trouble would gain you a shot at getting an interview from me. Correct?"

What the hell. Lee sighed. Her cover was blown, her ideas and plans were blown, and quite likely, if Ralt McLean so desired, her entire career could be blown. Two faint lines crossed her forehead as she wondered what the going price was for a story on balloonists? "At the time it sounded perfect," she said without the slightest embarrassment. She was beyond embarrassment, she thought dully, she was to the "wanting to crawl into a hole and die" stage.

"Exactly how did you know where to find me?" Ralt asked curiously. The more he studied the combination of lightly tanned skin, deep green eyes and dark curly hair, the more he found his anger abating. This was a damned pretty girl he was facing.

Girl.

He frowned again. She couldn't be more than twenty. What the hell was her family thinking, letting her roam around as she was doing? What if he and Raz were murderers, or sex offenders?

Come now, his conscience warned him. She's a reporter, and next to your hatred for sauerkraut stands reporters.

"I'm sorry, but I can't reveal my source," Lee said stubbornly.

"So you can't." Ralt nodded, his speech clipped. He turned to Raz. "Do your own checking when you get back to the ranch. If you get wind of anyone having shot off their mouth, fire 'em. Now, let's see if we can get Ms. Cantrell on her way."

A short time later, a very subdued Lee stood by and watched as each man tried to start the car and became more puzzled by the minute when all their efforts failed. They huddled, they swore, they poked and pried. Nothing worked. Finally, as dusk approached, Raz straightened from half lying beneath the hood and scratched his gray head.

"I'll tell you, Ralt. I think this damned thing has jumped time or the timing chain is broken."

"I think you're right." Ralt frowned, raising a hand

43

to the back of his neck, then flexing the tired muscles of his shoulders. He'd planned on spending the day relaxing. Instead he'd wound up playing mechanic to a damned reporter. There was no justice in the world.

He looked to where Lee was standing, a pang of conscience stabbing at him for the rude way he'd treated her. How could anyone as innocent as she looked be so full of trickery and deceit? He'd long ago decided that to be a "good" reporter, a person had to be a natural, genuine snoop. From every aspect, the word sickened him. There had to be something basically evil about a profession that profited on the misfortunes of others.

"Ms. Cantrell, I'm afraid only a tow truck can take care of what ails this buggy."

"But it's getting dark," she pointed out inanely. "I mean, surely you don't plan on leaving me out here by myself?"

"Well." Ralt appeared deliberately vague. "You could always wait for the balloonists to return. Perhaps you could signal them?" He grinned evilly.

"You know damned well they won't be back," she threw at him, finding herself heartily sick of Ralt McLean. Frankly, she couldn't see even the tiniest reason why America should want to read anything about him. He was rude, he was a boor, he was—

"Naturally, we'll take you to wherever you need to go." Ralt grinned mockingly. He liked her spirit.

"Oh," Lee murmured, caught unaware by the first decent gesture from the hateful brute. "That would be nice," she murmured stiltedly.

"I also think it would be nice if you would tell me exactly how you knew where to find me."

It wasn't exactly a threat, Lee decided as she stared at the huge man before her, but it did occur to her that he was her only means of transportation out of the brush.

"My best friend, of whom you've never heard, knew I'd been assigned the impossible task of interviewing you. Well," Lee shrugged, making no effort now to hide how weary and tired she was, "I'd been trying for days just to try and locate you." She regarded him resignedly. "You really are a pain to keep up with, you know. At any rate, Maria heard—on a date, at a cocktail party, on a Ferris wheel—I really haven't the faintest idea where, that you would be somewhere around Raymondville during the middle of the week, hunting. I happened to get wind of the balloonists and, knowing my boss's interest in that particular sport, decided to kill two birds with one stone."

"Well, Ms. Cantrell." McLean smiled, and Lee was amazed at the difference it made in his rough-hewn features. Why . . . it made him appear almost human.

"Well, what?" she asked, suppressing the eagerness —the excitement his smile was making her feel. Were the gods going to smile on her after all? It would be fantastic when she waltzed in and showed Cole what she'd accomplished. Yes indeed, Cole would quite probably fall off his chair with surprise. And the biggest surprise of all, she told herself, was Ralt McLean turning into such a malleable individual. From all

45

she'd read and heard about him, she would never have believed it.

"I never grant reporters interviews."

In her mind, Lee saw the bubbles bursting. She saw herself being pushed into the background while the other, more knowledgeable reporters got the plum assignments. She hadn't the slightest difficulty seeing Cole's expression of grim resignation when she told him that she'd failed.

Failed.

That one word kept skipping through her mind. She'd failed, and all because the infuriating ass standing before her had an uncommon hatred for reporters. At that precise moment Lee was positive she hated Ralt McLean.

"Never is a long time, Mr. McLean," she said determinedly. Suddenly an idea occurred to her. "Since you're obviously a betting man, what do you say to a little wager?" It was as bold a move as she'd ever made. She, an aspiring reporter, challenging a multi-millionaire without blinking an eye. Cole would have to give her something for courage.

Ralt glanced at Raz, then back to the pleasant pastime of staring at Lee Cantrell. Damnation. It was a pity she was a reporter . . . really a pity. But be that as it may, he still liked her style. She wasn't awed by his position and wealth, nor was she regarding him hungrily, as had become the boring habit of most women he met.

"Exactly what kind of bet do you have in mind, Ms. Cantrell?" he asked huskily, the timbre of his voice

46

catching Lee unaware and sending tiny shivers along the surface of her skin.

"I have two and a half months within which to do a story about you. You're the biggest thing to come my way," she looked him over from head to foot and grinned, "and I mean literally. At any rate, I don't intend to fail."

Ralt nodded, a smile of amusement on his rough face. "I admire your tenacity. However, I don't care if you're the mother of the Pope, or the sister of God, I won't do one single thing to help you. Therefore, a wager would be pointless. So why not do like everybody else and fake it?" he asked curiously. "This time, I won't even get mad."

"Because I abhor fakes, Mr. McLean," Lee quickly returned. "My boss is paying me to get the goods on the real Ralt McLean, and that's what I'll deliver to him on my deadline."

"You sound mighty positive," Raz entered the conversation. "I can't begin to tell you how many men and women I've had to throw off the ranch for having the same idea. Some even came in their motor homes and asked if we furnished hookups."

"May I ask why your boss is so interested in me?" Ralt continued, and for the first time since she'd burst upon them so abruptly, she detected a casual, laid-back feeling emanating from the man. He'd relaxed, and it changed his entire personality. No longer were the tiny, tense lines at the corners of his eyes exaggerated. His mouth had become less rigid, and Lee found her gaze going more and more to the attractive line of his sensuous lips.

She took a deep steadying breath, her green eyes touching on his mouth before colliding with his cold blue ones. "Er . . . He thinks you're misunderstood, and that the people deserve a chance to know the real you." She shrugged, trying to stop staring at him. Are you out of your gourd? her tiny voice of caution shrieked. Here you are, standing in the middle of a hot desolate stretch of nowhere, and all you think of is Ralt McLean's mouth. Why don't you try getting your insensible brain in gear and get the hell back to civilization?

"I see."

"He's also a stickler for the truth," Lee said simply. "That's evidenced by the success of his magazine."

There was that slight tightening of his features, Lee observed. She was dying to ask why he hated the press so. She even got far along enough to open her mouth to pose the question, then stopped. She'd pressed her luck far enough for one day.

"Tell me something, Ms. Cantrell. Do the stories you write about people make any sense or do you just fill in the pages with one or two twisted facts, a lot of innuendo, and the rest lies?"

"As I've already told you, Mr. McLean," she shortly replied, "I stick with the facts."

"That's nice . . . for you. Unfortunately it doesn't change my mind." He placed a large hand beneath her elbow, nodded to Raz, and the three of them began walking toward a small break in the brush and trees. Once through the break, Lee saw a blue pickup truck. In minutes, she was seated between Raz Cutlitt and Ralt McLean, and headed for civilization.

48

The feel of a hard thigh brushing against hers as the truck bounced over each bump reminded Lee of Cole's warning of how dangerous Ralt McLean was to the peace of mind of women. She slanted a look toward him out of the corner of her eye, feeling like a complete idiot that her heart was thumping along at an approximate ninety-five to a hundred beats per clip!

She saw the faint stubble of a dark beard, and thought how human it made the great McLean appear. She let her gaze move unhurriedly over the hard, unyielding line of his jaw and chin, inwardly delighted with the cleft in his chin. She wanted to touch that small indentation. Instead, she eased her hands beneath the backside of her thighs.

Her green eyes moved on to his wide, capable hands clasping the steering wheel. They and his arms were covered with a generous sprinkling of dark hair. Was it coarse or silky, Lee wondered. She was unaware of a deep sigh escaping her till Ralt glanced down at her and grinned.

"Something on your mind, Ms. Cantrell?" His bold gaze met and held hers. One could read volumes or one could ignore the obvious invitation and try to forget. Lee chose the latter.

"Of course, Mr. McLean," she said pleasantly, and without the slightest bit of conscience. "I was thinking of some chores I have to do in the morning. Nasty things . . . like cleaning the oven."

"Funny." Ralt chuckled. "I wasn't thinking of ovens at all. Want to know what I was thinking about?"

"No." She delivered that one word so forcefully, the silent Raz almost choked with laughter.

49

Thankfully, Ralt McLean only regarded her for a moment with those deeply blue and unbelievably cold eyes. When he looked back to the track in front of him, Lee drew a deep breath of relief.

Frankly, she would have given anything to be hundreds of miles away from the man seated beside her. She wondered what on earth Cole had been thinking of to send her on this assignment. In fact, she couldn't think of a single individual who was capable of handling Ralt McLean—not even Cole, and that was saying a lot.

Unfortunately, instead of that truthful thought bringing her any comfort, Lee felt defeated. Where she'd felt triumph a short while ago, there was now disappointment. She'd lost the battle—for the moment. But she wasn't through, she silently vowed. Not by a long shot. She was going to get her interview with Ralt McLean if it was the last thing she ever did.

CHAPTER THREE

"You did what?" Cole looked disbelieving, then took a big sip of the scalding-hot coffee he'd just poured. "Damn!" he muttered sharply, the back of his hand going to his mouth.

"You heard me," Lee remarked impatiently. "I scared off some huge beast called a Nilgai. What on earth is that anyway?" she asked curiously.

"I believe they were released in the Rio Grande Valley sometime during the thirties. The climate in the valley is not unlike that of their homeland, India. I understand they've multiplied till there's an impressive number of them now. They really are remarkable animals."

"Yes . . . well," Lee murmured skeptically, "I'm sure they must be if McLean is hunting them. At any rate, it seems he and his foreman had been wanting this particular Nilgai for months or years . . . or whatever. They were all ready to take a shot at the poor bugger when I arrived on the scene."

Cole shook his head, closing his hazel eyes for a moment. "It gets worse?"

"Yes. We got into a terrible row after he called me

51

an 'idiot woman screaming like a damned banshee.' From there things definitely went downhill."

Cole grimaced. He rubbed at his right eyebrow, a sure sign that he was in a quandary. "Well . . . an interview would have been nice, kid, but what the hell. It's not the end of the world." He glanced down at the scribblings on his calendar that no one in the world—including the CIA, Interpol, or the KGB could decipher. "How would you like to cover the wedding of Elvira Henderson to Albert Dolmain?"

At first Lee smiled. He wasn't angry with her. How nice. But the longer she stared at him, the more it became apparent that, though Cole didn't appear to be angry, he wasn't exactly doing handstands of joy either. And he was dead serious about the wedding.

"Who or what is an Elvira Henderson?"

"She's a quiet, unobtrusive individual making some extra bucks in one of the cottage industries—quilting. She lives out of town a few miles. I happen to think it's great if a person can utilize a hobby and make it pay off for them in their home. I also resent big business trying to take that right away from the individual. Ms. Henderson has persevered. I think it's time she got a little support."

"And you think an article in *Man's Viewpoint* will give her that boost?" Lee asked curiously. Cole had an eye for what would appeal to his readers. Lee had little doubt Elvira Henderson would find herself somewhat of a celebrity after the story ran.

"It certainly can't hurt her. She's definitely open to the idea."

"Ahh." Lee smiled. "Am I to ascertain from that

remark that you've already smoothed the path for me?"

"Actually, I'd planned on giving it to one of the others, but since the McLean thing has fallen through, you might as well have a go at this."

While he was talking, Lee was pulling at her bottom lip with the sharp edges of her teeth. She didn't care one bit for the way Cole was referring to her assignment on Ralt McLean as having fallen through. Not only was she still smarting from her disastrous collision with that individual, she had also been left with an unsettling feeling—as if whatever business there was between them had merely been placed on hold.

Don't be a ninny, her inner voice hooted in wild derision. You have no business with McLean. You can't get within a mile of the man, and you know it. As for unsettling, why not be honest and admit that you found him to be one hell of a sexy man? As rude a person as you've ever met, but sexy as hell nonetheless.

"Lee?" Cole snapped his fingers before her eyes. "Earth to Lee. Come in, Lee," he teased.

"Sorry," she murmured, chagrined, giving a quick shake of her head as she tried to dislodge the picture of a pair of ice-blue eyes. "My mind was on something else."

"I know," Cole muttered ruefully.

"What's that crack supposed to mean?" Lee shot back, embarrassed.

"Offhand I'd say it has something to do with Ralt McLean. He got to you, didn't he?"

"Certainly not," she lied without a hitch. "It's just that I don't like leaving something unfinished." She

53

paused for a moment. "What would you say to my hiring a private detective for a few days?"

"For what purpose?"

"To help me get some sort of schedule on McLean. I went around in circles for four or five days without ever once seeing him, till the hunting incident. When I inquired at the two most obvious places—his office and his apartment—you'd have thought I was a skunk about to spray stink on every available inch of space."

Cole stroked his chin thoughtfully. "A detective, hmm . . . ? That might not be a bad idea. Got anybody special in mind?"

"My friend, Harry Osgood, has built up quite an impressive reputation."

"If you think you can work with him, then he's your man. But, Lee," Cole said with quiet authority, "you can have Osgood for only a week."

"Cole," she protested.

However, he remained firm. "A week, Lee."

"What about the interview with Ms. Henderson?"

"I think you should do it. It's a good piece and you'll find her an interesting person. It's also an entirely different slant from a millionaire of Ralt McLean's stature."

"You make me sound like a snob." Lee frowned.

"Not at all. You're young, ambitious. That's the way it should be. Go after McLean by all means. I'd have been disappointed in you if you hadn't come up with another means of getting at him. But a word of advice—don't forget the Elvira Hendersons along the way."

54

Lee stared at him thoughtfully, her green eyes spar-kling. "You're very profound today."

"Just remember one thing. I would like an interview from Ralt McLean, but not to the exclusion of all else, nor do I want to see you hurt."

"Hurt? Don't be ridiculous," she quickly protested, feeling the hot flush of embarrassment stealing over her face. "What's there to hurt?"

"This mystique I spoke of when we were first talk-ing about McLean has been known to intrigue more than a few women, honey. I'd hate to see you become one of many."

Lee didn't respond. She honestly didn't know what to say. How could she tell Cole that Ralt McLean was the most intriguing man she'd ever met?

Later, while having lunch with Harry, Lee put her plan before him.

"How long do we have?"

"A week."

"A week!" he exploded. "Then there's no need wast-ing your time or mine. You should know by now that Ralt McLean moves like an invisible shadow. It'll take me longer than a week to even try and work up some sort of tentative schedule."

"That's better than what I have at the moment," Lee said slowly, her thoughts grappling with how she was going to keep Harry on the job longer than a week without Cole knowing. "Give it your best shot, Harry. Officially, you'll be working one week for *Man's View-point*. After that, you'll be working for Lee Cantrell . . . in case anyone asks you."

"In other words, Cole Taggart is holding very tight pursestrings, eh?"

"He wants the interview," Lee mused as if talking to herself, then related her run-in the day before with Ralt McLean and the silly bet she'd made.

"Well, don't let it get you down." Harry surprised her by grinning. "There are a couple of social events coming up here in the crescent city of which Mr. McLean is a patron. He never fails to put in an appearance."

"And of course you're invited to these functions." Lee smiled.

"Certainly," he returned with feigned haughtiness. "Have you forgotten the social position of the New Orleans Osgoods?" Harry came from a long line of bankers. His father still hadn't gotten over the fact that his son chose to be a private detective.

"Oh dear me, no." Lee sighed dramatically.

"I shall also be expecting you to accompany me to each of the forthcoming soirées, which you could easily attend with Ian and Susan if you weren't so stubborn."

"Never mind my brother Ian. You know we fight all the time. Are you sure your mother won't faint dead on the spot if you dare show up with a mere working girl on your arm?"

Harry appeared to be giving her remark special consideration. "I honestly can't say, my dear," he intoned in a fair imitation of Gayle Osgood's snobbish voice. "Seriously, you know she likes you."

"I do, but I couldn't resist the jab."

"So kind of you to accept," Harry dryly remarked

as he sat forward in his chair. "You're really just as bad, you know," he told her. "You're simply an inverted snob. You could travel in the same social circles if you chose to."

"Please," Lee implored him. "I hear enough of that from Ian. I honestly pity my sister-in-law."

"This is true," Harry agreed laconically. "However, Mom doesn't subject me to one of her lectures when I go out with you . . ."

"Mmm," Lee murmured. "Oh well, so much for our weird families." She rose to her feet. "If you need any more information give me a call. Need I say that I'm hoping you'll be unbelievably successful?"

"No. Busy this evening?" Harry asked.

"Chores. I'm doing the wash. To most every other woman that chore is relatively simple. They put their clothes in the machine, add detergent, close the lid and turn the dial to wash. At the end of the cycle, they remove the clothes. In my particular case, however, I'd be well advised to don combat gear, grab a chair and whip, then stand ready to rescue each item of material from the jaws of destruction."

Harry chuckled. "Still no results from the war of correspondence?"

"Nothing. Not a single solitary one or two lines on some vice president's letterhead. But I remain undaunted," Lee said determinedly. "This evening, I shall resume my efforts. Apparently, from what little checking I've been able to do, the company that manufactures and sells my washer is a small part of a huge conglomerate. You can rest assured I won't stop till I get to the head honcho of the entire outfit."

"Good luck." Harry laughed. "Keep me informed. It's one of the most amazing stories I've heard."

Elvira Henderson was a tiny birdlike woman with snowy white hair, twinkling blue eyes, and a ready smile on her lips that instantly put her visitors at ease.

The two hours stretched into three . . . four . . . five. When Lee took the brown paper bag from Elvira's small blue-veined hand, she caught a glimpse of her watch. Good heavens! It was almost six o'clock. She'd spent the entire day with the woman. She glanced about her, becoming for the first time aware of dusk having gently slipped into their midst and the gentle, sweeping countryside.

On impulse she leaned forward and kissed Elvira on one remarkably smooth cheek. "I can't remember when I've had a more enjoyable time," she said honestly. "And thank you so much for the jelly and fruit preserves."

"It was my pleasure." Elvira smiled. "You're a nice child. Come and see me again soon."

Lee stepped back, her gaze touching on the rustic walls of the large log cabin that had been in the Henderson family for generations, and the live oaks that sheltered it with their outspreading limbs. It was lovely.

The next few days were busy ones for Lee. She divided her time between working on the piece about Elvira which was going to be spectacular; her constant campaign regarding her washing machine; and the few facts she was able to uncover about Ralt McLean.

58

During the interval a letter arrived from Mr. Lowe, informing her that the proper course of filing a complaint regarding the performance of her appliance was to work through the local dealer. He also stated that he felt the washing machine she had purchased was their best seller. Was she sure she was following operating instructions that came with the machine?

After reading the letter, Lee was so angry she wadded the single sheet into a ball and threw it across the room. "Damnation!"

"I'll show them," she muttered after a few seething moments. She walked over to her desk and began searching for the piece of paper on which she'd taken notes earlier when she was talking with Maria. Maria, a legal secretary, had gotten her boss to make several phone calls regarding Lee's problem.

Ah yes, Lee smiled grimly, there it was. Ban-Cor, the manufacturer of her washing machine, was one of four companies controlled by a corporation by the name of Springcore, based in Chicago.

Lee immediately sat down at the desk, put paper in the typewriter and wrote a blistering letter to a Stanley Gunnison, the supposed head of Springcore. She was angry. After mailing the letter, Lee hurried back to her apartment and showered. She was going with Harry to one of the ritziest charity balls of the year, organized to help build a new wing on the children's hospital.

She and Maria had spent hours looking for the perfect dress. They'd found it at a small, exclusive shop, and Lee had almost fainted when she was informed of the price of the golden, shimmery gown. A tiny row of gold braid edged the bodice as well as the floor-length skirt.

"My God! This is terrible," she told her friend.

"Don't be silly," Maria said sternly. "You're hoping to make a connection with Ralt McLean, aren't you?"

"Connection—yes. Orgy—no," Lee reminded her. "And he definitely isn't picking up the tab for my wardrobe."

"Consider it ammunition."

"For what?" Lee asked, completely at a loss.

"Hunting the elusive McLean." Maria grinned devilishly.

"Only an interview with him, Maria, only an interview."

"Don't be deliberately obtuse. This will get you both." She held up the designer dress, the skirt long and willowy, the material whispering as it was moved back and forth. However it was the bodice that held Lee riveted.

"Maria, I'm no prude, but I simply can't wear that," Lee said quietly, fingering the two delicately pleated strips of material that rose from the waist, crossed in front and fastened behind the neck. That was all. Lee stared pensively. "Ian would have a heart attack on the spot. And even though I don't get along too well with him, I honestly don't want to see him in the hospital."

Maria laughed. "You are absolutely crazy, and Ian *is* a prude. However," she went on, "we can't be concerned with Ian. It's McLean we're interested in. Is Harry sure the man will be at this charity ball?"

"He'll be there all right. He's one of the biggest contributors."

She tried on the dress, protesting all the way, then stared at her reflection in the mirror. It was . . . daring to say the least. But McLean or no McLean, the dress looked like a dream on her.

"Having second thoughts?" Maria quipped, standing back, pleased as punch with the outcome.

"Don't crow," Lee told her. "I'm taking it."

Now, as she eased into the sheerest possible pantyhose, then took the dress from its hanger and stepped into it, she briefly closed her eyes against the silky texture of the material on her skin. Incredible! It felt as if she were being caressed from her ankles to her shoulders.

Harry stood transfixed.

Lee watched him over the silent laughter causing her body to shake. She was positive she could see the ends of his red riot of hair gently undulating from the effect of her attire.

"Am I to assume, by this stricken expression of yours, that you don't like my dress?" she asked with a straight face. He wasn't bad himself, she thought pleased, except that he looked terribly uncomfortable. She'd seen Harry in formal dress before, and each time he acted as though he were suffering from some mysterious disease that caused him to twitch, hitch, and generally look miserable.

Harry dragged his eyes from the criss-crossed bodice, past creamy shoulders tanned a light gold, on to a slender neck and to a face brimming with mischief. He saw a delicate line of bone, lightly arched brows, fiery green eyes and dark, curly hair. She was beautiful. She was also a friend.

How was that possible? Harry asked himself. Where had he gone wrong?

He shrugged one shoulder good-naturedly. "You'll do, kid," then laughed outright at the murderous look Lee threw him. He stepped closer and dropped a quick kiss on her cheek. "You look gorgeous, and you know it."

"Of course." Lee grinned cheekily. "But it never hurts to have your own opinion confirmed." She caught up a small gold clutch purse and her wrap. "Shall we get started?"

They laughed and joked all the way to the recently completed center where the ball was being held. Inside, Harry turned to her apologetically. "I hope you won't be too upset with me."

"About what?"

"My parents wanted us to join them at their table for the evening."

Lee smiled. "Relax, I don't mind at all." And she really didn't.

Sometime later, as they made their way back to the table from having danced a particularly fast number, Lee smiled at Harry. "I do appreciate the sacrifice you've made this evening, you know."

Harry squeezed her hand companionably. "Not to worry, toots. It's simply a matter of one maverick helping out another. In spite of the fact that you've been attracting men like bees around a honeycomb ever since we got here, I know you'd rather be at home in a pair of those awful jeans you insist on wearing."

"True." Lee nodded. "But this evening has had its funny moments . . . so far. Did you see Ian's face when he laid eyes on me? For a moment there I thought he was going to refuse to acknowledge me as his sister. When Susan said she loved my dress and asked to borrow it sometime, I thought he would choke."

"You shouldn't be so critical of Ian," Harry lectured her. "After all, he's your brother and he only wants the best for you."

"I think you and Ian have forgotten that I've been married and divorced, Harry. I don't need anyone looking after me."

"Point taken, but old habits die hard. Ian will come around some day. By the way," he went on in the same voice, "look to your right."

Lee did as he instructed, then felt her breath turn to lead in her lungs. Ralt McLean was standing talking to a group of people, but his eyes were looking straight at Lee. He'd been devastating in the rough hunting clothes, but in the black formal wear and stark white pleated shirt, he was incredible.

They reached the table too quickly. Lee was forced to turn her attention to Harry's parents. The older couple smiled fondly as they were joined by Harry and Lee.

"I do believe we'll reach our goal early this year," Mrs. Osgood remarked. "Everyone has been so generous."

"I'm glad." Lee smiled pleasantly. It took enormous

self-control to sit and calmly discuss the charity drive, when she was dying to turn and look across the ballroom. "I'm sure you've put in many long, hard hours on this event."

"I have." Gayle nodded. "But it's been a privilege. Tell me, dear. How are you liking your job at the magazine? I've been meaning to ask you each time we're together, but everyone gets to talking and I keep forgetting."

For one of the few times since getting to know Gayle Osgood, Lee found herself relaxing with the older woman as she answered her questions regarding her job. She wasn't sure if her relaxed state stemmed from her own self-confidence, the several glasses of wine she'd had to drink, or the certainty that before the evening was over, she would have talked with Ralt McLean.

When the warm, callused palm covered the pivotal point of her shoulder, and she heard the deep, husky voice speaking to the Osgoods, Lee found her gaze colliding with Ralt's.

"I hope you won't mind if I steal this beautiful lady for a few minutes." He inclined his head toward a cordial Harry.

"Only if the beautiful lady doesn't mind." Harry grinned.

Lee looked up . . . and up . . . and up. Her green eyes met the blue ones. It was as if time did indeed stand still. She saw the same craggy face, sheathed in granitelike hardness. This time, however, he was clean shaven. And though his voice was friendly enough, someone had forgotten to remind him that what one saw in his eyes was at odds with what he was saying.

"May I have this dance?" he asked, drawing her to her feet even as he spoke. He caught her hand in a loose, warm grasp and led her through the crowd.

"You didn't wait for my answer," Lee felt forced to point out to his broad back as he moved in front of her to prevent a slightly intoxicated man from running into her.

When they reached the dance floor, Ralt turned and folded her into his arms. Lee felt her heartbeat accelerate dangerously. Her breasts were pressed against a warm, vibrant chest, and his hands were on her back, locked at her waist. She wondered fleetingly if he could feel the trembling that was working its way over her body. "Were you really expecting me to wait for a polite nod from you?"

Lee looked up at him then, seeing a facsimile of a smile. "No, but it would have been the gentlemanly thing to have done."

"Are you a stickler for propriety, Ms. Cantrell?"

"Not at all. But then neither do I like having a relative stranger assume more than he should."

"Ahh." Ralt grinned. "The kitten has claws. Will it help if I apologize?"

"Are you apologizing?" she asked, enjoying the verbal jousting. He was heady as the wine she'd been drinking.

"Yes."

She tipped her curly head forward the barest fraction of an inch. "Then I graciously accept. When are you going to let me interview you?"

Ralt threw back his head and laughed, the sound of it drowned out by the noise of the band. "I don't believe this. I thought you'd given up."

"You're my biggest assignment to date, Mr. Mc-Lean," Lee told him pertly, "and I don't mean to stop until you've shared some of your deep, dark secrets with me. Have you forgotten my offer to make a wager on this?"

"Quite the contrary, Ms. Cantrell. I haven't forgotten a single moment of that afternoon. There are, however, secrets and there are secrets," he teased mockingly, "just as there are more intimate places in which to share them than the dance floor of a charity ball."

"Oh dear," she remarked facetiously, "is this where you invite me up to see your etchings, with the promise to grant me an interview at the same time?"

"Would you come?"

"No." Lee sighed. "I'm afraid I'll have to pass. Instead, we could meet in some quiet corner in the library."

Ralt stared incredulously, then laughed again. But this time when he looked down at her, Lee saw a gleam in his eyes, a faint warmth that hadn't been there before. "Is there some reason, of which I'm unaware, that necessitates you meeting me only in public places?" This incredible creature in his arms was turning an extremely dull evening into a fantastic one. His eyes dropped to the tempting bodice that revealed the soft curve of her breasts. It would be so easy to forget that Lee Cantrell was a reporter . . . too damned easy. She was exactly what he needed at this stage to add a little sunshine into his life.

"Of course. I've been warned that you mow women over by merely glancing in their direction," she said with an effort not to laugh. "You're supposed to trifle with their emotions and do heaven knows what to their bodies. From everything that I've read about you to this date, it would appear that for you to maintain this Herculean reputation with which you've been accorded, you would have to spend all your free time when you're not 'fooling around'—their words, not mine—doing nothing but continuously consuming some fantastic form of aphrodisiac. Now tell me honestly," she leered comically at him, "don't you think that would be an excellent opener for an article on you? I mean . . . look, it would grab the readers' attention, so to speak." They were acting like two kids, and she liked it. Who would ever have thought Ralt McLean could be so human?

Don't be so silly, the tiny voice inside her sneered. If he had appeared in full Apache war dress and dragging a dead buffalo, you would have thought it simply adorable! Haven't you figured out yet that you're attracted to the man? And can you even begin to imagine how utterly ridiculous that is?

Ralt gave every impression of considering her suggestion. "Only if I'm allowed to demonstrate my prowess at the library."

"I like that." She nodded, trying desperately to ignore the way his hands were caressing her back and shoulders. "Nice philanthropic gesture. When shall we start?"

"First light in the morning should be an excellent time. I seem to be at my best first thing."

"Now see?" she said saucily. "You answered each of my questions without having a single bad thing happen to you, Mr. McLean. Think how harmless the real thing could be."

"Call me Ralt."

"All right, Ralt. Most people call me Lee. As I was about to say, when are you going to give in and let me set up two or three appointments so that we can talk?"

Ralt watched the way she tipped her head to one side as she looked up at him. He was achingly aware of the softness of her skin against his palms, sending desire for her spreading out over his body. "Tell me, Lee. Why did you come here tonight?"

"Truth?"

"Please."

She raised her hands to rest on his chest just below his shoulders. "To get another crack at you, of course. Harry, my escort for this evening, says I'm an inverted snob. I suppose I am, but I've never really cared all that much for affairs such as this. My brother, who is also here with his wife, thinks I'm some kind of freak. If people want to contribute to the hospital, then why don't they just do it? Why not take the money spent in preparation of the ball and add it to the coffers? Then if they want to throw a party, do so. Why does one have to be hinged to the other? To me, it looks as if the ball is a cute little bribe for the guests having been good little boys and girls."

"You have some objection to people enjoying themselves?" Ralt grinned down at her, his deep voice creeping over her like an enchanted spell.

"Not really." She sighed. "It's just that I tend to climb up on my soapbox from time to time."

The music stopped, and Lee turned toward the Osgoods' table.

"Let's not go back just yet," Ralt murmured in her ear. He steered her through the maze of tables to a door set behind a barricade of greenery.

"You had no trouble finding the exit," she remarked as they walked out onto a wide balcony overlooking perfectly manicured grounds, "and I happen to know that this is the first affair to be held here since this center was completed. Did you send one of your underlings to case the joint before your arrival?"

"Of course. It's all part of my image." Ralt chuckled deep in his chest. He pulled her behind a wide, round column, and straight into his arms. "I'm going to kiss you, Lee Cantrell, and I don't give a damn if you print it on the front page of every paper in the world."

His lips, lips she'd been thinking about for days, took possession of hers with authority. His tongue found easy entrance into her mouth, for Lee hadn't the slightest thought of resisting him. She met his questing with her own, her head filling with the incredible sensation that she was floating. The fine hair on her nape stood on end, and there were goose pimples on her arms. She wanted to die from the feeling, yet at the same time, she wanted to live forever if it meant more kisses like this!

Hands that she'd looked at and admired were doing

the most delightful things to her. In one very faint second of clarity, she was aware of the feel of him beneath the bodice of her dress, of his palm gently taking the weight of her breast, his thumb lazily circling the pink nipple, then capturing the quivering tip and easing back and forth over its fiery surface till Lee was grasping at his shoulders, her knees weak and rubbery.

The sound of loud, merry voices caused Ralt to smother an oath, and also had him gently easing Lee away from him. He kept an arm at her waist, the other on her shoulder. "An interview with you might be the most enjoyable thing I've ever done," he remarked as he watched the way the shadowy light from inside played over her features. Her lips were slightly fuller than usual, and her eyes were languorous. His watchful gaze was measured, unreadable.

Lee slowly pulled her thoughts into some kind of order, more than a little subdued at how easily she'd handled the intimidating man standing in front of her, Cole's warning coming readily to mind. She put a still shaking hand to her hair and saw Ralt reach for it.

"Nothing's been spoiled," he coolly assured her, then released her completely. "I'm curious about something, though."

"What?" Lee managed.

"Do you always put such dedication on the line when you go after a story?"

Lee stared at him, hearing the edge of sarcasm in his voice cutting her like the edge of a knife. His eyes that had been showing a tiny flicker of warmth moments ago, were again as cold as ice. He'd gone from slightly human to a frozen semblance of a man, all within a few seconds.

"Perhaps I misread you." She lifted her chin in a gesture of protection. Damn him! "Being told that you not only consider yourself a financial genius but a super-stud as well, I naturally assumed the best way for me to get to you was through your libido."

Before Ralt could get another word out, Lee swung around on her heel and ran along the balcony till she found another door. She grasped the knob and opened it, not caring that the entrance was dark. She hesitated, able only to make out the long corridor to her right. She stood debating whether or not to take that roundabout way back to the main ballroom, when she heard the sound of footsteps coming toward her.

Lee hurried down the corridor, not caring where she was headed, just as long as it was away from McLean, the egotistical bastard! First thing in the morning, she was going to march into Cole's office and tell him there was no way she could work with the man.

A sudden, swaying movement had Lee quickly reaching out and bracing a hand against the wall. Wow! She'd had a couple of glasses of wine, but this was the first time she'd felt even the tiniest buzz. The world righted itself, and she started forward again. She hadn't taken more than two steps, when the door behind her was flung back against the wall.

"Lee!"

She threw a hurried glance over her shoulder and saw the outline of Ralt's powerful body in the opening. Damn him, Lee silently cursed, didn't he ever give up?

She hurried her step, the high-heeled sandals preventing her from breaking into an outright run.

"Stop, Lee!" Ralt yelled again, the sound of his heavy footsteps rapidly filling her ears.

"Go to hell!" she threw over her shoulder just as there was another wrenching motion that seemed to lift one side of the corridor at least five feet in the air. There was also the most incredible sounds all around her. Sounds that were confusing and not easily identifiable.

It hadn't been her wine at all, she concluded dazedly, then wondered at that totally crazy thought as she found herself being thrown toward the opposite wall. She threw out her hands in an attempt to soften the impact, and felt a sharp pain in her left wrist as it came in contact with the plastered wall.

"Lee?" she heard Ralt's voice behind her again. "Are you all right?"

Was she all right? she asked herself, her mind numb with shock, and her body bruised. "Yes . . ." she called out, but it was only a whisper. "Yes," she was able to yell the second time. "I'm fine. Are you?" Maybe a little bruising would do something to make him more human.

"Stay where you are, I'm coming to get you."

There he went again, Lee thought rebelliously, giving her orders. "No thank you, I'm perfectly capable of walking out by myself," she yelled back, only to have the words drowned out by the floor on which she was standing suddenly giving way beneath her, sending her on a jarring descent that ended with her on her knees.

Lee looked around in the near darkness in total bewilderment the same instant that a piece of wood glanced off the back of her head. She was aware of the dull thud of the blow, and even tried to put her hand to the spot. But her arms were heavy as lead and her hands refused to do her bidding. Darkness overtook her, and she slumped forward.

"Damn!"

There it was again, Lee thought fleetingly. Sounded like somebody was mad, didn't it?

"Can anybody hear me?"

She really did wish whoever it was would be quiet. She was sleepy, and it wasn't helping at all to have some noisy piker constantly moaning and groaning in the background.

But as awareness began to encroach upon her numbed brain, tiny, fitful tremors found their way to Lee's body. There also appeared to be an unbelievable cacophony of sound in the way off background. What the hell was going on?

"Lee? Lee, can you hear me?"

There it was again. So annoying. Couldn't she get a moment's peace around this damned place?

"Can you hear me, Lee?" The voice was urgent . . . desperate . . . even commanding. Lee's hand jerked at that commanding tone, dislodging some unknown piece of debris that made a clattering noise as it fell.

73

"Lee?" The tone was different this time. There was hope mixed in.

"Go 'way," she mumbled defiantly. "Wanna sleep."

"Lee! Wake up!"

"No."

"Yes, dammit! You're in danger . . . we're in danger!"

Something in the voice caught and pulled at her mind. She began struggling to sit, wincing as her arms came in contact with unseen sharp objects. "Wh-where are you?" she asked as she tried to focus her sleepy eyes, her palms rubbing at her arms. All she wanted was a nap. A silly little old nap.

"To your right, honey. Are you all right? Is there anything broken?"

Honey. He'd called her honey.

"Lee? Are you all right?"

Awareness began returning bit by bit while Lee sat looking all around her.

"Oh my God!" She put her hands to her mouth and smothered the scream ready to spring from her lips.

"Don't panic, Lee."

Ralt McLean! He'd been chasing her. Her mind was clear now, and began the not so pleasant task of remembering.

The floor they'd been walking on had collapsed. There was only a tiny beam of light coming through what had been a window, but there was a huge, gaping hole in the roof where stars could be seen. As she tried to deal with the outright panic threatening to smother her, Lee was aware that she could see outlines and shapes better than before the . . . whatever it was

74

that had happened. "Ralt?" She strained her eyes for a glimpse of him. "Can you hear me? Are you okay?"

"I can hear you, honey. Just don't panic. We may be here for a while."

"I can categorically declare here and now that of all the places I'd like to be 'for a while,' this definitely isn't one of them. I'm going to scream, Ralt. I can feel it coming."

Ralt tried to shift his large body so that he could see her better, but the dead weight across his legs wouldn't budge. Damn! If it hadn't been for him, she wouldn't be in this mess. "Hang on, Lee. Screaming won't help you at this point. Save your energy for later. Raise your arms so I can see you."

She did as he asked, then saw his own arm go up in return. "Can you move around?" he asked.

"I think so," Lee responded, then went about slowly flexing her legs, seeming almost surprised to find them still attached to her body. She put a hand to her chest, and was surprised to discover that part of the bodice had been ripped away, and one breast was bare.

How cute, she thought disgustedly. When it came her time to be rescued, she'd be shown on national television with one breast on display for the entire world. Ian would really like that!

"I'm mobile," she told Ralt.

He chuckled. "Good. Think you can work your way over to where I am?"

"Probably," she returned . . . "If I felt so inclined. However, at the moment I think I'll stay put."

"I need help, Lee."

She sat up straighter. This time there was no mistaking the seriousness of his voice. "Ralt? What's wrong? Where are you injured?" Not only was she talking ninety miles an hour, but she began moving like a small fury, pushing and knocking her way toward him. "Say something so I can get to you. Raise your arm again."

"You're headed straight for me, honey," Ralt told her. "Just be careful, please."

When Lee finally reached him, she simply stared down at the reassuring bulk of him, then promptly collapsed on his chest in a burst of tears. Ralt cradled her in his strong arms, his gruff voice murmuring comforting words in her ear.

"What has happened?" she cried, her tears dampening the front of his shirt, her voice close to hysterical. "What's going to happen to us?"

"We're going to be fine," he said sternly, his hands going to her upper arms and giving her a slight shake. "We're fairly warm, we aren't wet, and we don't have to worry about limited air supply. Understand?"

Lee nodded, her lips trembling as she tried to regain her composure for the third time that evening. "I'm sorry." She struggled to speak against the fear gripping her. "I'm not at my best when the floor I'm walking on decides to disappear. It does something to my self-confidence."

Ralt laughed softly as one large hand went out and brushed her hair back from her face. In the dimness he was beginning to be able to see better. He could make out the absolute terror showing in her face. It brought every protective instinct he possessed to the fore. His gaze dipped lower, to the creamy loveliness of one perfect breast. Without hesitating, his hand went out and covered it.

Lee didn't push him away. His hand was warm, and she told him so. "I didn't realize how cold I was till you touched me there."

"If you'll help me, I think I can get out of this jacket. That should take care of the problem nicely, don't you think so?" He spoke matter-of-factly, not embarrassing her in the least.

Lee murmured some inane response, and in no time at all she was snuggled in the warm jacket that smelled like Ralt. Suddenly it hit her. Ralt had remained on his back. He hadn't made any effort to come to find her or come to her earlier. Why?

She was sitting in the curve of his arm, and could feel the vibrations of his heartbeat against her drawn-up thigh. "Ralt?" She looked down at him, his name coming out in a near whisper. "Your legs. What's wrong with them?"

"They're trapped, that's all. I can wiggle my toes, and can even move my legs a fraction of an inch. There appears to be some sort of steel beam resting on the pile of debris on top of my legs. Fortunately, it isn't the other way around. I'll simply stay here till somebody comes along and frees me."

"Maybe I can do it," Lee told him.

"Don't you dare move," Ralt told her, his arm drawing her even closer. "There didn't seem to be too much danger for you to come straight to me, but we have no way of knowing what the floor is like in other spots. If you remember, we were on the second floor, and there's a basement. We didn't fall very far, so I can

77

only conclude we're resting on some sort of crawl space."

"Why hasn't someone come looking for us by now?"

"They will. I've been lying here listening to the sirens and all the hullabaloo going on across the way. From the sounds of things, there seems to be some pretty serious injuries. And even if we screamed our heads off, no one would hear us over all the other noise. We'll wait till it gets lighter, then we'll see about you getting help."

"I suppose you're right," Lee said on a shaky breath. "How could something like this happen?"

"Could be any number of possibilities. But the one that comes readily to mind is graft. Some money-hungry bastard cutting corners on proper building materials just to make a few extra dollars."

"If that turns out to be the case, then I'd sure hate to be in the contractor's shoes." She was silent for a moment. "I think I'll kill Harry Osgood when I get out of here."

"Your redheaded friend? Son of the banker?"

Lee nodded. "That's Harry."

"Is he the one who reminded you that I always attend this particular shindig?" Ralt grinned at her.

Lee stuck out her tongue at him. "Don't gloat."

"Who's gloating?" he asked with suspect innocence. "I think fate has played one hell of a trick on me, lady."

"How so?" she asked curiously.

"You messed up my day of hunting because you wanted that damned interview, you trailed me here this evening, and now here you are with me flat on my back. Did you have to destroy the whole damned building just for one lousy interview?"

"You're sick." Lee grinned at him.

"I'm also stubborn." He scowled. "I do not grant interviews."

CHAPTER FOUR

As the moments crept by, Lee began to detect a slight slurring in Ralt's speech. His arm around her hips became slack, then dropped away from her altogether. She kept talking, remembering having read somewhere that in circumstances such as she now found herself, it was imperative that the victim be kept conscious in hopes of forestalling or lessening the severity of shock.

She peered closely at Ralt's face, renewed panic assailing her as she saw the half-closed eyes and the problem he was having focusing.

"Trying to take advantage of me?" he joked, his head lolling to one side.

Lee grasped his chin in her hand and jerked his head around. "Listen to me, Ralt McLean," she said roughly. "I'll be damned if I'm going to sit here and allow you to pass out on me." Good God, she thought fleetingly, what was she to do? Ralt had been adamant in his refusal to let her go earlier for help. But what if . . . ?

"C-cold," Ralt stammered, his head now thrashing from one side to the other.

"Why didn't you say so before now," Lee scolded

80

him. She looked from the white pleated shirt, still relatively clean considering the circumstances. "I need to get your shirt off you, Ralt. Do you understand?"

"Y-you wan my sh-shirt?" He sounded drunk and disoriented, and Lee had to force back the panic building in her.

She framed his rugged face with her slender hands and looked straight into his dazed eyes. "Listen to me, Ralt. Ralt? Can you hear me?" she persisted.

"I-I hear ya." His voice was weak, hardly recognizable.

"Okay, Ralt. If you hear me, then try to help me raise you up. I have to get your shirt off and put your jacket back on you. Understand?"

He mumbled unintelligibly, but was remarkably cooperative . . . though somewhat uncoordinated in his movements. Lee struggled, she tugged, even cursed as she removed the shirt, then slipped long, muscled arms into the dark jacket and snugged it onto his shoulders.

With a sigh of satisfaction hinged on almost certain hysteria, she sat back on her heels and drew on the shirt, her fingers fumbling with the ends of the tail. She drew the two points to the front, tied them, then briefly closed her eyes.

God! What was she to do?

The noise surrounding the ballroom area was deafening. Sirens, screams, and complete chaos were still reigning. Lee knew she couldn't be heard above the din. But, she reasoned, neither could Ralt go much longer without medical attention.

She opened her eyes and looked about her, trying to

figure the best way to go. Apparently she and Ralt had been only about ten feet apart. But in the darkness, coupled with the total destruction, one had no way of knowing if they were stepping on something solid or if they would wind up in the basement, where the offices were located. Troubled green eyes looked back to the now quiet figure of the man beside her.

Ralt McLean.

He was a financial giant, yet at that precise moment, his money was useless. Lee sighed. She simply had to try to get him some help. He'd been rude to her on both occasions she'd been with him. Yet, in the end, he'd come after her without thinking of his own safety. After that first warning jolt, he could easily have vaulted over the balcony to the safety of the ground. But he hadn't, and she owed him.

Without further consideration, Lee pulled the front of the jacket together around him as much as its cutaway style would allow, then bent down and brushed her lips against the leathery cheek. "Take care, cowboy," she whispered. "I'll be back for you."

The antiseptic smell of the hospital caused Lee to hold her breath for a moment as she left the elevator and turned right toward room 3241. Hospital smells always made her slightly queasy. As she approached the door, out shot a harassed nurse.

The second her eyes fell on the visitor, the poor woman all but crushed Lee to her ample bosom. "Thank God!" she exclaimed. "You seem to be the only human being capable of handling him."

"I take it the patient is not in the best of humor

82

today?" Lee patted the nurse companionably on the shoulder.

"That's putting it mildly, Ms. Cantrell. He's absolutely livid."

"May one ask what prompted this latest outburst?"

"Somehow a reporter got past the guard and the nurses' station," the poor woman explained. "It was the sound of glass crashing that had us all rushing to Mr. McLean's room. We found the reporter backed up in one corner, a broken vase of flowers at his feet, and frightened out of his wits. Mr. McLean was slumped against the end of the bed with the bedpan cocked and ready to go toward his visitor's head. Thankfully, we got there in time and managed to subdue the patient and escort the guest out."

"And Mr. McLean?" Lee quickly asked, her breath catching in her throat. "Is he all right?"

"Well," the older woman shook her gray head, "the excitement caused his temperature to go up. He's still weak from shock and exposure, you know. Needless to say, all that activity didn't help his sore ribs either. He's very restless."

"I'll see what I can do," Lee promised, then walked on to the door of Ralt's room and went in.

"Well, cowboy," she briskly remarked to the scowling individual sitting against the raised hospital bed, his bronzed arms crossed over his chest while he glared at the world in general. He reminded Lee of one of his Indian ancestors. "Spreading your fatal charm, I see."

Ralt turned his dark head a fraction of an inch to include her in the outlying scope of his displeasure.

There was something rather comical about a man of his size reposing in a split-tail gown, Lee mused as she returned his unpleasant gaze with her own independent, amused one.

"Finally able to break away from your pressing career, Ms. Cantrell?" he asked sneeringly.

"For a few minutes, McLean, only for a few minutes." She walked on over to the table beside the bed, where she placed two new hunting magazines. "You might have read these, but I didn't know what else to bring you."

He barely glanced at her gift, his blue eyes busy drinking in the freshness of her, the saucy way her curly head was tipped to one side as she stared at him. Damn! She was one hell of a woman.

All the other females that had visited him during his five-day stint in the hospital—and there had been a number of them—had gushed and oohed over him till he was positive he was going to be sick. This one regarded him as evilly as the plague, and he was shaking in his boots with joy.

"Thanks. It's been a whole day since you visited me. Considering that you risked your own life to save mine, aren't you the least bit interested in hovering over me and watching each step of my recovery?"

"I don't hover, McLean, nor do I care to watch anyone as mean and ill-tempered as you." She reached for the straight chair upholstered in gold vinyl and pulled it forward a few inches, then sat down and regarded the patient with resigned forbearance. "If you continue acting like the royal ass that you are, you're going to be kicked out of this hospital."

"Ha!" he snorted, his dark, shaggy brows drawn together in a continuous line. It gave him a forbidding expression that served only to further amuse Lee. "Don't depend on it, kiddo. Two years ago I donated a quarter of a million dollars to this dump. At this very moment, I'm number one on their list of 'fantastic individuals'—their words, not mine—to be approached again for donations."

"In that case, try to have some compassion for the nurses. They don't benefit from your generosity, and your manners are appalling. The doctors may think they're gods, and they do prescribe the medication, but it's the nurses that do the actual dispensing, cowboy. If you've got an ounce of sense, you'll mend your ways."

Ralt was silent as he digested this blunt putdown. He tipped his great head back and stared at the ceiling, the wall, and finally at his visitor. "What's been keeping you so busy? Been seeing that Harry fellow?"

"I've had lunch . . . once with Harry. Since the accident, however, I'm something of a celebrity," she quipped sourly. "Getting credit for saving your obnoxious hide has made me into some sort of hero. I expect at any minute to be summoned to some official office and presented with a medal."

That brought a smile to Ralt's lips. "That bad, eh?"

"It's terrible, McLean," Lee confessed. "Every time I move there's a reporter lurking behind a tree." She regarded the entire length of him, still somewhat awed by his size. He really was the biggest man she'd ever seen. "How are you today?"

"So-so. My headaches are becoming less severe, and my legs are beginning to feel normal again."

"The nurse said you tried to pin a reporter to the wall with your bedpan," Lee teased him. "Bad choice of weapons, McLean."

"Sorry." He grinned back. "At the time that was all I could get my hands on. By the way, that was a very nice bit of journalism you did on the collapse of the center."

"How about the few words regarding you? What did you think of that?"

One broad shoulder lifted effortlessly. "It wasn't bad."

"Not bad, McLean?" Lee pressed. "You know damned well it was discreet . . . it was accurate without embroidering the accident. There wasn't a single word that wasn't the truth."

"All right," he said roughly. "It was okay. Is that better?" Frankly, he'd been surprised that Lee hadn't tried to make a big thing out of being responsible for saving his life. It would have gotten her a hell of a lot of free press, and boosted her career considerably. But nothing more than a brief account regarding him had been in the article, and Ralt respected her, even if he hated the work she did.

"No," she said just as nastily. "It isn't okay. But considering your mentality, I suppose that's about all I'm likely to get." She rose to her feet. "I can see you aren't in the mood for visitors."

"Where the hell are you going?" Ralt asked. Before Lee could blink an eye, he reached out and grasped her by the wrist. He didn't want her to leave. She was soothing to be with, he reasoned pettily . . . for a reporter. "I want to talk to you."

"Really?" she asked derisively, jerking her hand out of his firm clasp. "Then ask, McLean. It's a very simple procedure, you know. I'm a human being, you're a human being. In these days of modern miracles, it's possible for us to communicate by speaking nicely to each other, rather than barking or grunting or yelling like our ancestors of the cave era."

After a long, pregnant silence, Ralt said silkily, "May I please have a few minutes of your time, Ms. Cantrell?"

"Why certainly, Mr. McLean."

"Please." He patted the side of the bed. "Won't you sit down? Here, on the edge of the bed. It makes my head hurt when I lay on my side."

"Of course, Mr. McLean, I'd be happy to oblige you." She did as asked, then smiled brightly at him, throwing herself wholeheartedly into the game, even though she was itching to box his arrogant ears! "Exactly what was it you wished to discuss with me?"

"Would having an affair with me create any serious problems for you at the magazine?"

Lee stared at him as if he'd suddenly sprouted two heads, each equipped with ten horns. "Why do you ask?" After several speechless moments, she managed the question in as level a voice as possible. The gall of him! The incredible gall of him! He'd asked the question in the same manner he would have used in ordering a hamburger, fries, and a shake!

"Oh," he said, shrugging, finding it hard not to laugh at her subdued expression of outrage, "it's time to make some changes in my personal life. And even though you're a reporter, I think you have integrity.

All in all, I'd say we have a fair chance of making each other reasonably happy . . . for a while."

"But only for a while . . . of course."

"Of course. Marriage isn't for me. Twice was enough."

"Soured you forever on the idea, hmm?"

"That's about the size of it."

"How is it possible for you to want to go to bed with me, when you know so little about me?" she asked sweetly, her hands tightening into clenched fists. God! She could kill him.

"What's there to know?" What had he known about any of the women he'd slept with? And yet, he mused, there definitely was something different about Lee Cantrell.

She wasn't intimidated in the least by his wealth and position, and he liked that. "We've been thrown together under some very unusual circumstances, and each time you've revealed something about yourself that I like. Believe me, honey, for two people to make love, it's not necessary for them to know each other's life histories."

"McLean's Rule, I'm sure." Lee nodded, one corner of her lip caught between the edges of her teeth.

"Of course."

"Then I'd like to add that, if you'll look further, you'll find that most monkeys and apes also share your views regarding sex, McLean. They look, they grunt a couple of times, then get right down to the business of copulating. Unfortunately for the sake of your suggestion," her brows zapping together in an angry line above the bridge of her small nose, "I happen to be

88

neither. Not to mention the fact that I don't play by anyone's rules but my own. So take your offer and stuff it."

"I'm crushed," Ralt remarked piously, partly amused, yet annoyed that she hadn't taken the time to even pretend to consider his proposition. "Do you find me repulsive?"

"Quite the contrary," Lee returned stonily, her green eyes hard as flint. "I find you to be the complete ass."

"I'm extremely wealthy."

"So you are."

"Even a short association with me would benefit you tremendously. I'm a very generous man."

"How kind of you. I'm sure the women you've known have been pleased by your generosity."

"You still aren't interested?"

"No."

"I'll have to delve deeper then. There has to be something you want from me."

"Oh there is," Lee said honestly. "But without any strings attached."

"Honey," Ralt said softly, roughly, "I haven't done anything without some kind of string attached since I was sixteen. However, I'll humor you this once. What do you want?"

"An interview."

He frowned. "Even for you, I won't do that," he stubbornly maintained.

"Honey," she mimicked him, "I didn't save your egotistical ass just to have you sit there and refuse me an interview."

They stared at each other, each assessing, each pondering the next move. So far, neither had gained even so much as a decent inch against the other. But instead of disgust, there was respect mingled in with the wariness.

"You're a gutsy little thing, aren't you?"

"My ex-husband used to think so," Lee threw in, then held her breath as she saw Ralt grasp the words and absorb them. He was too much of a fighter to reveal his true feelings, she decided. But even with his superb enigmatical approach, she detected a slight flicker of surprise in his blue eyes.

"You don't seem old enough to have an ex-husband, Lee Cantrell. Tell me about him." Damn, Ralt swore to himself. He didn't want her to be involved with another man . . . emotionally or physically. There was something in her eyes when she mentioned this ex-husband. What was it?

Why? his conscience asked. Can't you stand to face the competition?

Competition hell, Ralt silently cursed. There wasn't a woman living he couldn't have if he set his mind to it.

Then why don't you stop acting like a jackass and try, once in your life, to really get to know a woman beyond how well she suits you in bed?

Her answer caused him to stop arguing with his conscience. "I think not. As you said, some very unusual circumstances have thrown us together. But even those occasions haven't seen either of us revealing much of ourselves. You'll find, McLean, that I'm a very private person."

Ralt regarded her narrowly, recognizing a bluff when he saw one. Trouble was, he shrewdly acknowledged, he found that for once in his life, he wasn't interested in winning each and every hand this new and fascinating game was dealing him. He would much rather learn more about the lovely woman sitting on the edge of his bed, who, in spite of being very much a part of a profession he detested, was as sexually attractive to him as any woman he'd ever known. He wanted Lee Cantrell, and he meant to have her.

"Do you still want an interview with me?" he asked.

Lee tried to hide her surprise, but knew she hadn't succeeded when she saw the faint glint of amusement in Ralt's eyes. His capitulation had been totally unexpected . . . especially at this particular point in their relationship. She'd already accepted that, in all probability, the interview would never become a reality.

So why have you continued visiting Ralt McLean? her conscience asked.

The only answer Lee could come up with was that she found him to be the most vibrantly alive man she'd ever known. When she was with him, it was as if each second, each moment was supercharged. Lee was completely fascinated by the man.

"Yes."

"I'm expecting to be dismissed in a couple of days. Would you like to be my guest at the ranch for a weekend . . . or for however long it takes to get the information you need?"

It was all Lee could do to keep from jumping into the air and clicking her heels together! She, the most junior member of *Man's Viewpoint,* was going to get the first-ever interview given willingly by Ralt Mc-Lean. She could hardly believe it.

"I've never been on a ranch." She was unable to hide the excitement in her voice, but there was also a sense of disappointment as well. Frankly, she was thinking, she was terrified of horses and cows. But surely she wouldn't be expected to do any riding . . . would she? "Other than cats and dogs, I'm not very fond of animals."

And what about the electricity running between you and McLean? Will you be able to handle that, living in the same house? Remember all the stories of his women that you read when you were first beginning your research on him? Will you become one of those women . . . one of the McLean castoffs? Knowing the incredible fascination this man holds for you, can you honestly expect to keep the relationship on a platonic level?

"A ranch is no different from any other place," Ralt assured her in a gruff but gentle voice. He found he was fascinated with the way the light in her eyes changed as frequently as her thoughts. His gaze slipped downward to the gentle thrust of her breast, then narrowed as he remembered the fullness of that satiny mound in his palm the night of the accident, and the way the moonlight brushed the rosy tip with its gentle brilliance.

"I also haven't thanked you properly for saving my life. The doctors have assured me that if I hadn't been rescued when I was, it's possible the weight on my legs could have left me with severe circulatory problems, as well as doing damage to the nerves. It took guts to pick your way through that rubble, especially when you weren't sure from one minute to the next whether or not you were going to fall twenty feet below onto a concrete floor." He caught her hand and squeezed it. "No one's ever made that kind of sacrifice for me, Leslie Elaine Cantrell. In fact, no one's ever made any kind of sacrifice for me. I won't ever forget that."

"Please don't try and make what I did anything more than one human being trying to help another. You would have done the same for me, wouldn't you?"

"Of course." Ralt nodded his dark head. "But the difference is, I didn't and you did, and I was the one who benefited from your efforts. That's pretty tough to forget, honey."

"You seemed determined to make me into a hero."

"In my opinion you are one."

"Why do I get the impression that you've become suspicious of most good deeds that come your way?"

"Because good deeds usually *don't* come my way without several distinct strings attached."

"I'm no different," Lee pointed out to him. "I want that interview with you very much."

"But I'd already turned you down," Ralt reminded her with a devilish grin, and it occurred to Lee, as she stared at him, that she'd seen him smile more during the last few minutes than all the other times she'd been with him.

Lee favored him with a pert grin. "Okay, so I'm a fantastic person." She preened comically, then slid off the bed. "Unfortunately my boss doesn't think I'm fantastic, so if I want to keep my job, I'd better be getting back to work." She touched a smoothing hand

93

to the leather belt emphasizing her slender waist. "Is it posing any difficulties for you, being hospitalized here in New Orleans rather than Houston?"

"Not really," Ralt told her, then completely surprised her by reaching out and opening the drawer of the nightstand and removing a leather pocket-secretary. He took out a card and handed it to Lee. "Those are the telephone numbers where I can usually be located. I'll trust you not to pass that information around."

"I wouldn't dream of doing such a thing," Lee said simply, and Ralt believed her.

Hell, his conscience scoffed disgustedly. You'd believe anything this broad told you. Wake up, this is a female—a female reporter. Can it get any worse?

"Do me one small favor before you go," Ralt said suddenly.

"Name it," Lee smiled confidently.

"Kiss me."

"What?" She looked startled. Surely she'd heard wrong.

"You heard me," he said silkily. "Kiss me."

As if her body were independent of her mind, Lee found herself obeying the outrageous command. She moved closer to the bed, unbelievably self-conscious as she placed her hands on either side of his head and bent down to brush her lips against his. But instead of letting her get by with the chaste peck, Ralt had other ideas.

His large hands held the back of her dark, curly head, and kept it immobile as his mouth opened beneath hers and his tongue became a hot, burning force, forging its way along the tender plain of her lips, across the ivory surface of her teeth and into the dark smoothness of her mouth. Her own tongue met the exciting intruder, and Lee felt the numbing rush of blood in her veins, leaving her weak and breathless. One hand went to the small of her back, the pressure causing her breasts to become molded to his chest.

This is Ralt McLean—the infamous Ralt McLean where women were concerned—Lee's more coherent thoughts kept shrieking out at her. Don't be foolish, she was warned. But somehow, as she fought against the maelstrom of desire caressing her, she knew there was more at stake than just an interview. Would her heart survive unscathed as well?

CHAPTER FIVE

During the remainder of Ralt's stay at the hospital, Lee visited him twice. By then he'd graduated from the split-tail gowns to pajama bottoms. It never failed to throw Lee for a loop when she would enter his room and see him naked from the waist up, the coal-black hair on a golden-skinned chest looking very sexy. She would stare just above his right shoulder when she talked to him, rather than at that part of his anatomy that was so pleasing to the feminine eye. If she hadn't actually seen him in a collapsed state, she would swear he was pretending to be ill for some nefarious purpose. He positively glowed with good health.

On the first visit, she found Raz Cutlitt with his boss. The older man was delighted to see Lee, practically wringing her hand off with his appreciation for saving Ralt's life.

"Please," Lee tried to shush him, her face turning a delightful shade of pink. She glanced at a grinning Ralt, who was infinitely aware of her discomfort and that she was becoming more embarrassed by the second. "How can I convince you people that what I did was very ordinary?"

Raz puffed out his chest like an insulted rooster. "Well now, Miz Cantrell, I don't see how you can stand there and talk like that. I know there's some bad blood between you and the boss there," he nodded toward Ralt, "but saving his ornery hide was a mighty wonderful thing to do. Me and the rest of the fellows at the ranch are mighty grateful to you, honey, mighty grateful."

"That's mighty generous of you all," Lee murmured amusedly. She looked over at Ralt, thinking how well he looked, considering what he'd been through. It was hard to believe that only days ago he'd been in shock. "How's the star patient doing today?" She fairly jumped at the question, hoping it would throw the mighty Raz off her trail.

"Fine," he said stiffly, all humor wiped from his face as he regarded her down the length of his considerable nose.

"Something bothering you, McLean?" She could see that his hair was still damp from the shower, and that he'd nicked himself while shaving. He looked and smelled divine to her.

"Why didn't you come by last night or this morning?"

"I went out to dinner last night," she said softly but clearly. "And this morning, I was putting the finishing touches on an interview I did a couple of weeks ago." She walked closer to the bed. "Was there something in particular you wanted?"

"Yes!" he snapped. "I wanted you."

"Really?" Lee smiled coolly, though the emotion reflected in her eyes was far from pleasant. "Then I suggest you remember a conversation we had recently, McLean. You're not a caveman, and I'm not your woman. You don't snap your fingers and expect me to jump. Understand?"

"When did it get to be such a crime for a man to want the company of a beautiful woman?" Ralt demanded gruffly, completely changing tack and throwing her off stride. Damn, but she was a feisty little thing, he thought. After years of living in a world where none of the women he dated had nerve enough to openly disagree with him, Lee Cantrell was proving to be as refreshing as a spring rain.

"To my knowledge it isn't," Lee was gracious enough to reply. "Is that what you really wanted?"

"Yes. I was lonesome," he sniffed pettishly, assuming a martyred expression as he stared up at the ceiling.

Lee and a highly amused Raz exchanged knowing looks.

"I think it would be best if I left, now that I see you looking so fit and robust." Lee smiled. She glanced down at the papers scattered over the bed. "I'm sure Raz hasn't come all this way just to visit you for a few minutes. From the looks of all this work, the two of you seem to have a full day ahead of you."

Ralt reached out and caught her hand. He glared at her but refrained from verbally attacking her. He'd learned, he reflected, that if he took potshots at Ms. Cantrell, she promptly loaded her own gun and fired right back. "You will come back by this evening?" he asked pointedly in what Lee assumed to be his most charming manner. However, the man had much to learn about the gentle art of wooing a woman.

Lee flirted with the idea of telling him that she was busy, but for some reason she refrained. "I'll come by on my way home from work."

"What time is that?"

"I usually leave the office around five."

"I'll expect you by five thirty."

"Even you, with all your millions, can't control the ungodly traffic in New Orleans." Lee gave the grinning Raz a rueful glance. "How do you stand working for someone as dictatorial as this character?"

"Oh," the shaggy-haired foreman looked down at the toes of his boots, then back at Lee, "you get accustomed to his ways after a while."

"Ha!" she scoffed. "That'll be the day." She removed her hand from Ralt's grasp and began moving toward the door. "See you later." She inclined her head toward Ralt. "Raz, it's been a pleasure seeing you again."

"Same here, Miz Cantrell. From what Ralt has been telling me, it appears we'll be seeing lots more of each other."

"Oh? You mean the interview?"

Raz nodded. "I understand you're gonna be our guest for a few weeks at the ranch."

"A few *days,* Raz," she laughingly corrected him. "I'm writing an article, not a book."

"We'll see." The foreman nodded, leaving Lee wondering curiously at the remark.

Back at work, Lee found her thoughts straying to the patient in room 3241. She first tried reviewing all the reasons why she shouldn't give Ralt McLean more than the usual interest afforded the subject of an article. He was a womanizer. He was a hard, cynical individual. He trusted no one. In a nutshell, he was the complete opposite of what she felt she really could respond to in a man.

On the other hand, there *was* that spark of attraction between them that had grown steadily with each meeting. All the things Ralt was became unimportant when they were together and the verbal sparring between them began.

Lee sighed. She couldn't define her feelings where the arrogant cowboy was concerned, and it annoyed her. Since her divorce from Lance, she'd prided herself on having excellent reasons for each step she'd taken in her life. She knew she wouldn't be happy till Ralt McLean was neatly categorized and labeled . . . and quite likely labeled dangerous at that . . .

"The piece on Elvira Henderson looks great, kid," Cole's rough voice interrupted the mental abuse Lee was heaping upon her head. He walked on over and leaned against her desk, staring at the work in front of her. "There is such a thing as overediting, you know."

"I want it to be perfect. She is a fantastic person, and I can't thank you enough for sending me to her," Lee confessed, not bothering to look up from where she was scribbling in the margin of the last and final paragraph.

"What a nice surprise." Cole chuckled. "Only days ago I was a monster. Now I'm quite lovable."

"Don't get carried away," she warned him as she dropped the pencil, then leaned back in her chair and regarded him with feigned haughtiness. "Lovable, you ain't."

Cole grabbed a handful of his rumpled shirt front. "I'm crushed."

"Good. You need to be brought down a notch or two. By the way, I'll be leaving tomorrow or the next day for McLean's ranch. Since I've never been further from this or any other city, other than that little jaunt to Elvira Henderson's log cabin, I have no idea what to expect. Will I need to rent a car? And even though he's asked me to be a guest at the ranch, would it be better for me to stay in town and drive out to the ranch each day?"

"By all means stay at the ranch," Cole told her. "I'm sure every propriety will be observed by your host, considering he's been dodging the matrimonial bullet for a number of years now. As for renting a car, play that by ear. If you would feel more comfortable having your own transportation, then feel free to rent one. On the other hand, you might find 'town' no more than one or two stores, a hole-in-the-wall restaurant, a post office, and a hardware–feed establishment . . . or even worse."

Lee rolled her eyes expressively. "My cup runneth over."

"A little country air might do you some good. Birds, crickets, coyotes, snakes."

"One more word—" Lee glared at him "—and I won't budge a damned step."

Cole reached out and deliberately ruffled her hair, knowing that action would rile her further. "You're a big celebrity now," he teased. "The phone hasn't

101

stopped ringing with people from other publications, the radio, and TV wanting to have you as a guest. Saving Ralt McLean's behind was a brilliant move on your part, kid."

Lee stared up at him. "You're incredible, do you hear me? Incredible. I did not save McLean deliberately." She shook her head in frustration. "The man was already slipping into shock, Cole. He was trapped and couldn't move. Of course I had to help him."

Cole patted her shoulder. "Don't worry, Lee. I'm proud of you. Subscriptions are flooding in with each new batch of mail. They're up nearly thirty percent and still rising. How about having dinner with me this evening to celebrate?"

"No thank you," she said stiffly. "I have other plans."

"No harm done. In the event I don't see you before you leave, keep a sharp eye out for McLean. He can be dangerous with women . . . or so they say. Personally, I haven't the vaguest idea who 'they' are, but their opinions do get around with considerable haste."

Lee had to laugh. "I should be resigning, you know. I'm a city girl, and you've done nothing to boost my sagging confidence but tell me to be wary of insects, animals, and reptiles . . . with and without legs." She reached out, caught his hand and squeezed it. "Thanks for having faith in me, Cole."

Cole grazed her chin with his knuckles. "You deserve good things, kid. You're a hard worker, and you're dependable. Keep in touch." He gave her a sketchy salute, then was gone.

Lee sat in her chair for several long, soul-searching

moments, staring into space and thinking. She was about to embark on a totally new and different aspect of her career. She only hoped she was capable of carrying off the assignment without becoming personally involved with the subject.

Her visit with Ralt later that evening showed her yet another facet of the complex man who had become her constant mental companion. She hadn't been in his room more than ten minutes when Raz arrived, his arms loaded with packages, followed by a young man similarly laden. Lee watched in amazement as the foreman whisked a small round table from behind the door, whipped a white tablecloth from one of the packages he'd set down, and spread it over the table.

"Sorry about the paper plates, Boss, but these are real sturdy." The older man shot Ralt a resigned glance. "Could have gotten dishes from the cafeteria, but you said you didn't want any damned hospital garbage." He motioned the young man forward, then began setting out huge steaks, large, fluffy baked potatoes, salads, French bread. "The nurses also balked at your order for wine. Said the strongest thing you could have was iced tea. I'll just set the apple pie over here."

Lee looked from Raz to Ralt, her expression one of total disbelief. "How on earth do you expect to get away with this?"

"It's simple." Ralt grinned. "I had Raz buy steaks for every member of the nursing staff on this floor, on this shift."

"You bribed them," she said flatly.

"That's how you get most things in life, Ms. Cantrell," he said with deliberate sourness. "Everybody has a price. And when that price is met, then that person belongs to the one who's paying. It's that simple."

"It's despicable, you mean," Lee fumed.

"Er, excuse me, Miz Cantrell . . . Ralt," Raz broke into the heated conversation, all the while edging toward the door. "I think me and Raoul'll mosey along. See you first thing in the morning, Ralt."

After the door closed, Ralt lowered his feet to the floor and waiting slippers, shrugged into a navy blue robe, then pulled out one of the two chairs at the table. "Will you please join me for dinner, Ms. Cantrell?"

It would serve him right if she'd turn on her heel and leave him, Lee thought, but she didn't. Instead she got her temper under control, and then was glad she'd stayed. In addition to the most delicious steak she'd ever tasted, she and Ralt talked and laughed for the better part of an hour.

"So you still see your father-in-law, or should I say former father-in-law?" Lee asked. Somehow they had gotten off on friends, and how some friendships could survive the worst strain, while others crumpled at the hint of unpleasantness. Ralt had just finished explaining how Douglas Nelson had given him his big break, and how he respected the man. She was also inordinately curious about his relationship with Nelson's daughter, who had been Ralt's second wife. Had their marriage been a happy one?

"You mean since Sally's death?" Ralt asked bluntly, seemingly not in the least perturbed by the question. The expression in his blue eyes was enigmatic as he regarded her across the small table, leaving Lee to shift uneasily, wishing she'd couched the question a bit more subtly.

"I'm sorry," she said honestly. "I didn't mean to bring up something so obviously unpleasant."

"If anyone else had brought up the subject, I'd have told them to go to hell. But with you, it's different."

Never one to leave a stone unturned, Lee frowned. Why was he willing to be so open with her? Had he felt the same inexplicable pull between them that she had? Surely not. No . . . Certainly not. It was only her imagination.

"Is something bothering you?" Ralt asked, seeing the uncertainty flickering over her face. "Is something wrong with the pie?"

"Nothing is wrong with the food, it's delicious, and I'm stuffed," she answered truthfully.

"But?"

Lee hesitated. "This is very difficult to explain."

"There have been moments in my life when I've been told I'm a very understanding man," he said in his deep, gruff voice, an infectious grin teasing his sensuous lips.

"I just bet you have," Lee retaliated cheekily, responding to his mood. "Okay, here goes. Even though we're having dinner, and nothing has been mentioned about the interview I'm going to do, I somehow get the feeling that you're giving me information about yourself that you wouldn't ordinarily hand out, because of what you think I did for you. I mean . . . You shouldn't." She lifted her hands in confusion . . . "What I'm trying to say is that I'm not out to get you to reveal things about yourself and your loved ones

105

that will hurt you, McLean. I know there are certain facts about me, and events in my life, that I would never reveal to someone for the purpose of them putting the information in print . . . not that anyone would ever want to." She shrugged. "Nevertheless, I'd like—above all else—for our relationship to be an honest one. I could never take advantage of what you think you owe me."

"I understand." Ralt nodded. "And I assure you, I won't tell you a single thing that I don't want to. Okay?" God, McLean! You are going down for the third time, and you're too stupid to try and save yourself, the tiny voice inside him whispered mockingly.

"Fine."

"May I finish telling you about Sally?" He cocked one eyebrow quizzically.

"Certainly," Lee managed levelly. Actually she was on tenterhooks for him to get on with the story, but she hoped she wasn't looking quite as desperate as she felt.

"Sally was Douglas Nelson's only child. She was a sweet, tomboyish kid who had a crush on me from the first moment she set eyes on me. Unfortunately she grew up to be a sweet, tomboyish woman who *thought* she was in love with me. She wasn't demanding in the least, and we would probably have been divorced in another year or so if the unkind hand of fate hadn't intervened."

"Why did you place so much emphasis on the word 'thought'?"

"Because Sally was in love with the idea of love. She was a dreamer, one who tended to take life as it came

106

and managed to enjoy every minute. Her death was an outrage of the worst kind and totally unnecessary," Ralt said harshly. Lee could see the fires of anger jumping in his eyes, and felt the hair on her arms standing on end.

"I'm-I'm sorry," she stammered after a moment or two, unsure of what to say to the fiercely angry man facing her.

"Be sorry for Sally," Ralt murmured harshly. "She was a very nice person. Unfortunately, we should never have gotten married."

"Other couples often make that same mistake," Lee offered inanely. "I admire you for not saying your wife didn't understand you."

Ralt took a sip of iced tea, then grimaced. "As a matter of fact, Sally didn't understand me. She thought I was a nice person."

"I'm sure that's because she loved you. And when you forget yourself and let go, you are a very nice person." Lee smiled at him. "Your Sally must have been a very discerning lady."

"But not a wise one. I was all wrong for her. As I said, we were headed for divorce."

She regarded him consideringly. "But you wrote the book on stubbornness, and it's my guess you'd hang in there till some workable solution was reached. No," she mused almost to herself, "I don't have you tagged as a quitter. I really don't think you'd walk away from someone you loved."

"Neither do I, Ms. Cantrell," he replied mockingly. "Neither do I."

. Lee swallowed uneasily, then looked down at the

partially eaten piece of pie in front of her. Okay, she told herself, now you know that he didn't love his wife. Are you happy? Is that revelation going to make one particle of difference in your life?

"Cat got your tongue, Lee?" Ralt softly taunted. "Do my confessions make you uncomfortable?"

"Yes." She looked up then, forcing herself to meet the cold, enigmatic gleam in his eyes. "Frankly, they make you sound like a cold, hard person without an ounce of caring for another human being."

"That depends on the human being, honey. Now with you, I know for a fact that I could build a fire that would singe that curly hair on top of your pretty little head. Once we get to the ranch, I'll show you in more detail what I mean," he easily drawled, making Lee's palm itch to slap his arrogant face.

He was the most exasperating man she'd ever met. One minute she was fascinated with him, and the next found her enraged by his arrogance. And yet, Lee floundered among the many conflicting thoughts slipping in and out of her mind at the moment, he'd been painfully honest regarding himself, never once uttering an unkind word against his wife. Was he always so blunt?

An interview was one thing, Lee decided, and she was determined to get it. But what was the price she'd have to pay?

CHAPTER SIX

Lee looked about her as she sat down next to the window. It was the first time she'd flown in a small plane, and she had definite reservations about the matter. She pinned Ralt with a hard look as he dropped into the seat beside her.

"Is there some problem?" she asked, her voice betraying her nervousness. He'd been talking with the pilot, and Lee, her pessimistic mood in full throttle, was positive they would crash on take-off or shortly thereafter.

"Yes." Ralt nodded gravely. He leaned toward her and fastened her seat belt, then his own. He eased back, his gaze lingering on her mouth. "There is definitely a problem."

"Then why the hell are we moving?" she demanded, ready to tear the seat belt loose if necessary.

"How else do you expect the plane to fly if we don't take off?" He grinned at her.

"I don't *expect* anything but to get out of this thing," she hotly informed him. "Exactly what sort of difficulty are we having?"

Ralt assumed an expression as innocent as a baby. "None that I know of."

"But you implied the pilot had a problem."

"He does."

Lee clenched her teeth together in frustration, her eyes briefly closing as she considered the avenues of escape available to her. Realizing there were none, she inhaled deeply, then looked at the grinning ass beside her. "May one inquire as to the gentleman's problem?"

"Certainly." Ralt nodded so agreeably, Lee wanted to murder him. "He bought some new heifers last week. One of them is sick, and he was asking my advice."

"Heifers?" she repeated incredulously.

"A young cow."

"A cow . . ." Lee repeated in a dazed voice. "You mean to tell me," she began, her voice gathering momentum with each word, "that you've had the nerve to sit there and let me nearly have a heart attack thinking there was something wrong with this plane, when all the time you and your pilot were discussing a few mangy cows?"

"You'd better not let Harv hear you speak so disparagingly about his babies." Ralt chuckled. "He considers them the first love of his life." Before Lee could guess his intentions, he dropped a long, hard arm across her shoulders and drew her against his warm body. "We Texans, ma'am," he began in his best western drawl, his head close to hers, "don't take too kindly to having our cattle downed."

The scent of him and the feel of him was too potent.

110

Through some weird and inexplicable twist of fate, Lee was finding herself becoming more and more attracted to this McLean character. Something had to be done . . . and quick, she thought frantically, else she was liable to end up with a sizable crack in her heart.

She forced her slightly shaky fingers to the task of removing a manila folder from the slim briefcase resting on her lap. "I don't think I want to talk to you for a while, McLean." She turned and frowned at him. And the moment she looked into his eyes, she realized how dangerous that was. "I don't like having dirty tricks played on me. Especially ones wherein I'm terrified of my certain death by falling to earth like a damned rock."

Ralt's bottom lip was caught between the strong edges of his white teeth as he regarded her with open amusement in his blue eyes. "You aren't kidding, are you?"

"Not in the least." She shook her head, and tried to force her body to relax. "I'm not the bravest soul in the world when it comes to flying anyway. Then when I saw the size of this plane, and assumed from your remarks that there was some mechanical problem, I panicked."

As she talked, Ralt felt the temperature of his body rising to unbelievable heights, and knew it hadn't a damned thing to do with air conditioning! Even the sound of her voice on the telephone had him wanting to crush her in his arms and make love to her. Perhaps being in such close contact with her during her stay at the ranch would give him a better insight into her personality, show him some flaw in her character that

111

would banish the perfection with which he now viewed her. His feelings where she was concerned caused a portion of his life to be out of sync, and that annoyed him.

Lee turned her attention to the letters in the folder, feeling the almost instant rise of her blood pressure as she reread the excellent job each man had done in passing the proverbial buck. "Cowards," she muttered in an almost inaudible whisper.

"Problems?" Ralt asked. He too looked at the file, catching the names of men with whom she'd been corresponding, and a couple of the companies within the corporate ladder that she'd managed so far to unearth.

"And how," she returned grimly, then related the story of her fantastic washing machine, her efforts to get it attended to, and the total lack of cooperation shown thus far by the companies involved. "If I had the time to ferret out the weasel, I'd go straight to the top man on the totem pole. He should know exactly how business is being conducted by one of his companies. On the other hand, I doubt he cares as long as the profit margin is what he wants. At any rate," she lifted her hands expressively, "not only am I the owner of an appliance that is totally unpredictable, I'm also out nearly a hundred dollars in clothes and linens. But aside from all that, it's the principle of the thing. I resent the way they've continued to pass the buck without doing a damn thing. The warranty on the machine won't last forever, and I just bet you they'll be quick to inform me of such a thing when and if I try to call in an independent repairman."

"Would you like for me to see if there's some way I can expedite matters for you?"

"No."

"Ahh." He grinned. "I can see that you're after blood. Right?"

"At least a kick or two on the shins." She returned his infectious grin with her own attractive smile. "This," pointing to the letters, "has become an obsession with me."

Ralt laughed. "I can tell. Just out of curiosity though, what would it take to soothe your ruffled spirit?"

"Letters of apology from all these wimps, a new washing machine, and reimbursement for the items of clothing and linens that have been ruined. After that, I think I'll talk with Cole about doing an article on how housewives, the greatest testing group in the world, are duped by manufacturers. Naturally I would recount my own personal story as well as giving the name and make of my washing machine."

"You know," Ralt said slowly, "I've never thought of it in terms quite like that. Probably it would make an excellent story. If you do talk your boss into it, I want a hand-delivered copy of the story."

"*Man's Viewpoint* is an excellent magazine; you should subscribe to it," Lee told him, trying to speak naturally around the lump of excitement wedged in her throat. "After all, my interview with you will be coming up before too long."

"Oh . . . I already get the magazine," he baffled her by admitting. "Wanting you to personally deliver

113

the article is purely selfish on my part. By doing so, I'll know you're thinking of me."

Lee ducked her head, knowing she was clearly out of her depth as how to best deal with this man. McLean gave new meaning to bluntness of speech and manner. He'd made it abundantly clear that he found her attractive and that he would like to go to bed with her. She'd never had a man say such things to her. Make passes . . . of course. Immediately after her divorce, when she'd first begun dating, she'd grown accustomed to dealing with overamorous men. She'd gradually weeded out the obnoxious ones, and spent a great deal of her social hours with steady, reliable Harry.

But what do you really think of the proposition? the tiny voice inside her whispered. There's been no one before or since Lance. Have you matured emotionally to the extent that you could handle an affair with the likes of this cowboy? If not, then you'd be well advised to run. McLean is not a man to give up on something, once he sets his mind to it . . . and it definitely looks as if he's set his mind on you, honey.

"Do you think of me, Lee Cantrell, when you aren't with me?" The voice was low and husky in her ear. It sent simultaneous shivers of hot and cold scampering over her.

"Y-yes." She nodded. "How could I do otherwise? I've been studying everything about you and your accomplishments I could get my hands on, in preparation of doing this interview." What a copout! What a huge crock! She thought about him before she went to sleep at night, and that wasn't part of her research.

"That's not the same thing, and you know it." He scowled. "What you've just described is called 'doing your homework.'"

He pulled back to his own seat, maneuvering his large body sideways so that he was facing her. His arm was still behind her shoulders, and the tips of his fingers were making feather-light forays against the tender, sensitive sides of her neck and into the edges of her dark, curly hair. "I'm greedy," he said openly, not the least embarrassed to be discussing something as intimate as their making love together. "I want to be the most important thing on your mind."

Lee somehow managed to meet the direct challenge in his eyes, her skin tightening at the husky caress in his voice. "From what I've been able to learn about you, cowboy, you wouldn't want to be the most important thing on my mind for very long. Right?"

Ralt shrugged. "Let's just say, I'm not known for my staying power when it comes to women."

"At least you're honest about it." She was grateful that he wasn't fool enough to try and convince her that he found her to be the most fascinating woman to come his way in years. At least he credited her with having some common sense.

"Does that turn you off?"

"No . . ." she drew a deep breath, her heart almost beating through the walls of her chest with a sense of nervousness . . . a sense of excitement. An excitement that had been building inside her from the moment she'd first met Ralt, and had been steadily increasing since she accepted his invitation to join him at his ranch. "No, it doesn't turn me off. In fact, I much prefer it that way."

Ralt's hand left its idle torment of her neck to cup the pivotal point of her shoulder, his touch hot and vital through the silky material of her emerald green dress. "Let's get back to that question I asked you when I was in the hospital. Do you remember?"

Lee smiled, the motion bringing a certain mischievous gleam to her eyes that, at that precise moment, were the same smoky green as her dress. "Are you really serious?"

"Yes."

"Of course I remember. It's not every day that some man suggests I share his bed for a while."

"You're making it sound cheap," Ralt said after a moment of quietly watching her. Dammit to hell! It was happening again. Every time the subject of making their relationship a more personal one came around, it was as if his image were projected as some lecherous ass. Yet regardless of how his suggestions portrayed him, he told himself, he was still infatuated with Lee. At moments he felt as though someone had slipped him a mysterious drug, its effect . . . to reduce his powers of thought and self-protection, leaving him an easy prey for the beautiful Ms. Cantrell.

"To some people, it is," she said honestly. "You've asked me to sleep with you. Wasn't too long ago that a woman who agreed to a proposal such as yours found herself with a very besmirched reputation."

"And you, Lee? How do you feel about sleeping with me?"

"That's a difficult question," she said thoughtfully.

116

"Because of what we've survived together, I feel a closeness with you that's unique. Yet it's circumstance that has thrown us together not the more natural, social process of getting to know one another. In answer to your question, I frankly don't know."

"Come now," Ralt pursed his mouth mockingly. "You're acting as if this is something new to you. You've been married, and I'm sure you've had your share of lovers since then. I refuse to believe you don't know the score by now."

"Married? Yes. Been another man's mistress? No."

"Okay." Ralt lifted his hands dismissively. "Wrong choice of words on my part. I'm sure you've been intimate with other men since your divorce. The point I'm trying to make is, why act so shocked when I suggest that we enjoy some time together?"

"Do you think all women go about satisfying whatever sexual urges they might have with the same disregard as you're accustomed to doing?" Lee asked curiously.

"The women I know do. Frankly, I don't see anything wrong with it, I assure you. Double standards, when it comes to morality—as well as several other subjects—make no sense whatsoever to me."

"How generous of you," she cooed innocently, the knife-edged gleam in her eyes not at all in harmony with the sugar-coated tone of her voice. "And of course you're quick to assure all those women who do wish for a little . . . er . . . fun, that you'll be more than happy to accommodate them?"

"I don't make myself a public stud, if that's what

117

you're getting at," Ralt said in his usual plain-spoken fashion.

"Yes . . . well." Lee inhaled deeply, the heat in her cheeks accompanied by a brilliant shade of pink. "Flying in a small plane is very interesting." She changed the subject to halt the blushing.

"Indeed," Ralt said. "In fact, I can't remember a single occasion in the past when I've found it so satisfying."

Lee darted a quick suspicious glance at the carefully masked features and into the eyes that seemed to be reading her like a book. She turned and stared out the window of the plane, feeling the safe, steady rules, by which she governed her life, slipping irrevocably from her grasp. The days ahead held the promise of . . . Lee's saner, more down-to-earth part of her mind took command, refusing even to consider what the days to come held in store. She had a feeling it would be best to take each day at a time where Ralt McLean was concerned.

The ranch was everything Lee expected it to be and more . . . much, much more. Raz met them at the airstrip, located on the south side of the ranch, in a dusty jeep, his weather-lined face wreathed by a huge smile.

"Welcome to the ranch, Miz Cantrell," the foreman greeted her, catching her slim hand between both his callused palms. "It's a pleasure to have you here," he informed her without slowing down the steady pumping of her arm. "Yes, ma'am, a mighty big pleasure." He released her hand, then clapped her on the shoulder with such force Lee was positive she was going to wind up with her nose buried several inches in the bare earth on which she was standing.

Ralt, who had been standing by during the exchange, decided it was time for him to intercede. He reminded the older man of the luggage. "I'm afraid Raz tends to become rather effusive when he genuinely likes someone," he chuckled close to Lee's ear. "Is your shoulder broken?"

Lee grinned as she flexed her right hand and arm. "I think I'd better get me a mighty thick suit of armor, pardner, if I'm to be a frequent recipient of Raz's affection."

As she spoke, she let her gaze run briefly over the undulating countryside. She'd never seen anything so vast in her entire life. To her right could be seen the hub of the ranch built on a gradual rise, comprised of the sprawling Spanish-style house laid out in the form of a squared U, and the numerous buildings set some distance away. The vastness of this land surrounding her at the moment was awesome—totally in concert with the towering man beside her, and equally as intimidating.

Ralt watched the play of emotions flitting across her face, and felt a certain let-down feeling assail him. For some inexplicable reason, he'd wanted Lee Cantrell to like the ranch as much as he did. He'd expected the light of excitement in her eyes, not the expression of bewilderment he was seeing.

"You're very quiet."

She tried to smile, determined to put the ghost of her thoughts and contradictions behind her. This was simply another assignment. Ralt McLean was simply another man. One who had faced tough, seemingly insurmountable odds in his life, then forged ahead and made his fortune. "All this," she gestured ineptly. "It's . . . it's overwhelming."

"And peaceful."

"And lonesome."

"And beautiful."

"And spooky as hell. How far are we from town?"

"Why town's just a hop, skip, and a jump over them hills over there." Raz nodded to the west as he walked back to the jeep with the last of the luggage. "But you won't have much call to go into town, honey. Why, the peace and quiet of this place will lull you to sleep as peacefully as being in your mammy's arms. There's nothing as pretty as the sunrises, unless it's the sunsets. Then there's all that open space." He waved one long arm toward the vastness Lee found so overpowering. "Why, a body can go for miles . . . for hours and never see another human being. That's what makes this country great. You don't feel hemmed in."

"Exactly how far is a hop, skip, and a jump?" Lee asked with a sinking feeling. How was she to have known, when she supposedly saved Ralt McLean's life, that she would wind up in this godforsaken place? She knew without even asking that horses would come next. Could an interview with a man of McLean's importance be conducted within twenty-four hours? Twelve hours?

"Nigh 'bout twenty miles," Raz told her.

Her response was drowned out by Ralt's loud,

120

"Let's get moving, Raz," followed by him cupping her elbow and hustling her into the jeep.

The talk between the two men on the way to the main house was mostly about cattle and cattle and more cattle. Some were confined to a holding pen, away from any other of the livestock. They were new arrivals at the ranch, had clean bills of health, but it was a practice of Ralt's not to allow new stock to mingle till they'd proven they were clean. There were cows to be moved from one section of land to another. Some were to be vaccinated, others were to be rounded up and sold. Feed that had been bought several months earlier and was stored in silos in another part of the state was discussed. Lee was at a loss to understand how any four-legged creature could cause such an uproar. If they were so damned pesky, why did people want to fool with them at all?

"Are they this much trouble all the time?" she asked as soon as there was a lull in the conversation.

"What's that, ma'am?" Raz asked, puzzled. Ralt looked at her as if she'd gone stark raving mad.

"Cows. From listening to the two of you talk, it appears you do nothing but play nursemaid to cows. And please, Raz, call me Lee."

"Why, Miz Cantrell . . . I mean, Lee!" the astonished foreman exclaimed in his rusty voice, his face turning even ruddier as his thoughts were conceived faster than his mouth was able to transmit them. "That's what ranching's all about. Without them pretty things out there," indicating with the wave of a hand a small herd of holsteins grazing in a pasture, "what on earth would we do?"

121

"Find a nice steady job that wouldn't keep you up all night or out in the icy snow and rain during winter."

"Lord love her," he spoke fervently, his disbelieving eyes staring at his boss. "Ralt, this is serious."

"Take heart, Raz," Ralt drawled in his husky voice that sent goose bumps flying over Lee's arms. "Ms. Cantrell isn't much for the outdoors. If the earth isn't covered with concrete, she thinks something is wrong. We'll change her mind before she leaves us," he said confidently. His arm, heavy across her shoulder, tightened, drawing her close for a quick hug. Lee pushed against him, annoyed with them for making fun of her.

"I may be a city girl, but at least I don't spend the greater part of my life talking to cows," she retorted archly.

That remark led to another . . . and another . . . and another, till Raz recovered from shock, Lee got over being teased, and Ralt was left with the strongest determination ever of seeing to it that the lovely creature sitting beside him would—someday—come to think cows were the most beautiful sight on earth.

Why does it matter to you what the woman thinks? his conscience asked.

Ralt stared into the space as his strong, tough body was jostled by the roughness of the jeep and the wind ruffled the thickness of his dark hair. He wasn't exactly sure why he wanted Lee to like the ranch, or why he wanted to be absolutely certain that she liked him, but he sure as hell felt that way and he didn't plan on fighting the urge one iota.

CHAPTER SEVEN

From the moment Lee stepped from the jeep, walked beneath the limbs of an old, gnarled oak tree and through the front door of the house, she felt the graciousness and warmth of it reaching out to her like a gentle presence. She paused, unable to break the spell slowly spreading over her, her gaze moving from one area to the other in rapid succession.

The floor was dark, and made of wide planks, polished till one could see a dull reflection of their features against the surface. The same dark wood was used approximately three feet up the walls, then the remaining expanse to the ceiling was painted a soft cream. Handwoven Indian pieces were shown off to perfection by the starkness of the color scheme, as well as other artifacts native to the area. Lee stared at an especially striking piece of sculpture on a small mahogany table, depicting an Indian brave with arrow aimed, astride a horse. From the detail and exquisite craftsmanship, she was positive it was a Remington. To the left of the foyer she caught a glimpse of the dining room, and to the right, the more formal setting of a living room.

"It's lovely." She smiled up at Ralt, who had been watching her with an expression of such anticipation that Lee felt her heart melt. Before she could say more, the housekeeper joined them.

Grace was in a terrible mood and wasted precious little time relating her grievances to Ralt.

The older woman, her slender figure clad in a neat print dress, and her graying hair tightly permed, was in a royal snit. Her small, gold wire-rimmed glasses rested halfway down her nose as she stared at Lee. "First time in a long while that you've brought a woman home with you. Pickin' 'em kind of young these days, aren't you? Well you better decide what you're going to tell that Carrie Warren. She's about to drive me crazy, hanging around here all the time." She peered closer at Lee. "You two planning on marrying or is it just a sexual relationship like couples are having these days?" she blurted out even before Ralt had a chance to make the introductions.

"Watch your mouth, Grace," Ralt said without the least bit of censure in his voice. "This is Lee Cantrell. She's here to do a story about me for a magazine called *Man's Viewpoint.*" He looked down at an amused Lee. "This is Grace Masters, my housekeeper. She has atrocious manners and a mouth that needs washing out with lye soap. Otherwise, she's a kindly soul in some ways."

"Miz Cantrell," Grace said in response to Lee's nod, her dark brown eyes darting over the newcomer with open curiosity. "Ralt, you know you hate reporters. How can you stand there and lie like a dog?"

"He's telling you the truth, Gracie," Raz added his

two cents' worth as he came in with the luggage. "Lee's the one that saved his life."

"You better not be bringing sand in this house, Raz Cutlitt. Just take those bags on to the room I cleaned yesterday." She turned back and smiled at Lee. "Well why didn't you say so in the first place?" She took a step forward and caught Lee's hand in a bone-crushing grip that rivaled Raz's. "That was a mighty neighborly thing for you to do, honey," she crooned, "mighty neighborly."

Lee smiled, struggling not to laugh as she met Ralt's amused glance. "Really, it was nothing."

"Ha!" Grace snorted. "You're just being modest. Raz told me all about what happened. Yes sir," she shook her head, "you're a hero in these parts."

"Anything else on your mind, Grace?" Ralt asked, once he'd rescued Lee's hand from the exuberant grasp of the housekeeper.

"Well in addition to that aggravating girl worrying me to death, there's some senator that keeps calling here—something to do with you agreeing to help him catch illegal aliens. Surely he's mistaken," Grace added pointedly. "I told him that you wouldn't be stupid enough to get involved in that mess again."

"Josh Emmett." Ralt nodded. "He's not mistaken, I have agreed to try to get the other ranchers in the area to band together in an attempt to try and curtail the alien situation by refusing to hire them and to report any suspicious movements among their own hands. The next time Emmett calls, I want to talk with him."

"Tangling with the people who deal in human flesh is a risky business," Grace muttered ominously.

Ralt patted her consolingly on the shoulder, assured her there was nothing to worry about, told Raz he would talk with him later, then caught Lee's elbow and began hurrying her toward double doors that led into a spacious hallway running right and left.

"Raz and Gracie have been with me for years," he explained as he turned to the right, then back to the left and began walking down the one side of the U. "I'm afraid they're more friends than employees. Sometimes they tend to be a bit bossy."

Lee grinned. This was the sort of thing she knew the public wasn't aware of when they heard the name Ralt McLean. And frankly, neither was she. For who in the world would have pictured the cowboy being chastised by an ageing housekeeper and an equally elderly foreman? It made him far more approachable, she decided.

"I think it's very nice of you to humor them the way you do. It's obvious they care deeply for you."

"I suppose you could say that. They're about all the family I've got," Ralt said thoughtfully. "At least I think of them that way." He stopped before a darkly stained door, opened it, and gestured for Lee to precede him.

A low, throaty groan of pleasure came from her as she stood in the center of the large, airy room. All the furnishings appeared to be antiques. But it was the bed, with a rose and cream canopy, that caught and held her attention. All her life she'd wanted to sleep in a bed with a canopy. Her delighted gaze went on to the other pieces. The overstuffed chaise covered in a tiny rose and cream-colored check. A slipper chair in splashy greens and rose, a desk and chair made of cherry wood, and a dresser with a marble top and a beveled mirror. Rather than carpet, there was a large oval braided rug on the floor, and the walls were the same as those in the rest of the house.

Lee looked over her shoulder at Ralt, who was standing just inside the room, an expression of wariness etched in the hardened features of his face. "At the risk of sounding redundant, may I say it's beautiful? As a matter of fact, everything about your home that I've seen is beautiful."

Ralt walked over to where she was standing, not stopping till he was directly in front of her, his broad chest lightly brushing the hardened tips of her breasts. He let his arms rest on her shoulders. "I like having you in my home, Lee." His eyes were warm and glowing, drawing Lee into the labyrinth of emotion she'd come to associate with this man.

He touched the side of her face with his fingertips, and she was amazed anew by the gentleness that could come from him. It occurred to Lee that Ralt went to great lengths to give the impression that gentleness was an unknown quantity in his makeup. In fact, during their brief but unusual relationship, she'd begun to suspect he was one of those individuals who equated gentleness and love with weakness. But during the accident, she'd gotten a better look at the real man behind the façade . . . He roared like a lion, but was a pussycat underneath. He was an immensely powerful individual. The day-to-day decisions he made controlled countless lives. Yet Lee had a weird notion that she'd seen a side of Ralt McLean that had never been revealed to another living soul. That intrigued her.

Instinctively, she pressed her face against his touch, unable to explain the surge of need forging a bridge between them. Her gaze openly merged with his, and one part of her wanted his touch . . . wanted to feel the roughness of his hands over her entire body, not just her face. It was a wild, totally insane thought, but one she was finding more and more difficult to deny. The other part of her warned her to remember Lance. By following her feelings before, she'd been instrumental in ruining two lives. Hers and Lance's.

"McLean . . ." she began hesitantly, "I'm not sure I'm ready for this."

Ralt sucked in his breath, his eyes taking on that same cold, hard glaze Lee had seen on their first meeting. "Are you still in love with your ex-husband?" Even as he asked the question, Ralt felt the cold hand of fear squeezing his heart.

Knowing she'd shared the special intimacy of marriage with another man had been eating away at him for days now . . . which was, he was quick to admit, crazy as hell. Yet, even if she still loved her ex-husband, Ralt knew it wouldn't change the way he felt about her. Without even trying, she'd woven a spell around him that he was powerless to break. In his heart he knew that until he'd sated his desire for her on every level, he wouldn't be able to regain control over his own life.

"I still care very deeply for Lance," she said honestly after several thoughtful moments. "Contrary to most divorced couples, we still like each other. We even see each other occasionally."

"Then may one ask why a divorce was necessary in

such a blissful existence?" Ralt asked mockingly. He made no attempt to release her, not wanting in the least to make her explanation easy. It was as if something inside him were pushing him, urging him to exploit each and every second he was alone with Lee.

"We found that love wasn't enough. At least not the kind of love we felt for each other," she explained.

"Which is about as clear as dishwater."

"Lance and I dated in high school and were married while we were still in college. He was the captain of the football team, I was a cheerleader. We thought we were in love but what it boiled down to after a few short months, were overactive libidos and an association that had become very comfortable. Unfortunately, neither affliction was enough to save our marriage."

Ralt was silent as he stared down at her. Honesty. The word kept spinning in his head. She was one of the few women he'd known in his life who was honest. He found it to be a virtue he treasured.

"I could stand here all day and tell you ten different ways that I'm sorry that your marriage didn't work, but I'd be lying." He allowed his arms to ease down over her and draw her snug against him. She was warm and soft and he was aching with the need to make love to her. "If your marriage had lasted, I'd never have met you." He grinned. "I'd also have a very nice trophy for my wall. On the other hand, who would have been there to save me when the building collapsed on us?"

"I'm glad you didn't kill that poor animal. Besides that, I looked up pictures of that particular critter, and it has to be the ugliest creature on God's green earth.

It's a mystery to me why you'd want its ugly mug hanging on your wall. As to saving your worthless neck, McLean, if you hadn't been chasing me," Lee said softly, lifting her face to the searching magic of his lips as they teased and touched her face, "you wouldn't have been in the hallway at that particular time."

"This is true," Ralt murmured on a raspy breath. "And yet, I'd have been willing for the Empire State Building to fall on me if it meant having you save me."

"You are a masochist." Lee smiled dreamily.

"Mmm . . . I also remember the feel of your breast in my hand. That rosy little nipple reminded me of a tiny, tightly curled rosebud." He maneuvered his hand between them, then eased his fingertips to one turgid tip and then the other. "See?" he said huskily. "They haven't forgotten at all."

The sound of quickly indrawn breath, followed by a pleasurable sigh was the only sound in the room. Lee's hands crept up to clasp Ralt's neck as she tried to draw him even closer. Being in his arms had her poised on the razor-edge, her emotions were taking over. She knew her fascination for him could be dangerous, but she was caught in a passionate realm of slight fantasy or insanity and she ignored all warnings. She shocked herself as she graphically pictured what would happen if she continued to play with the highly flammable McLean, but she couldn't control herself when he spoke to her or touched her.

Her thoughts caused the color to rise in her cheeks but before she could pull away in embarrassment, Ralt released her. The slight smile on his face hinted at a deeper satisfaction within him. "I'll leave you to your unpacking, Ms. Cantrell." He stepped around her and began walking toward the door, pausing with his hand grasping the knob. "By the way, I'm extremely curious to hear more about your former husband."

"Why?" Lee asked, equally curious as to why he had questions regarding Lance.

Weren't you nearly dying to hear about his wife? her conscience reminded her.

"He was another man in your life," Ralt remarked levelly. "From what you've told me about him, apparently a part of him is still there. I don't like competing with a ghost."

Lee's own gaze was just as flinty as she countered his remark. "If that's what you really think, McLean, then why bother? And just to set the record straight, Lance is anything but a ghost. In fact, if you'll turn on your TV set this evening, you can see him."

"He's an actor?"

"No. He's Lance Porter, quarterback for the California Wingers. They're playing the Pittsburgh Cougars this evening."

Ralt nodded thoughtfully. "A sports jock, mmm?"

"Not at all," Lee answered crisply. "He simply enjoys football. He's also a fourth-year med student, and plans to specialize in sports medicine."

After staring at her for several long moments, his gaze as enigmatical as ever, Ralt left the room.

"And a good day to you, Mr. McLean," was Lee's cryptic murmur as she gave a slight shake of her head, then walked over and stared out the French doors. Beyond a lovely flagstone patio, bordered with lush green plants, was a huge swimming pool. A quick glance to the right and left showed that the pool and patio appeared to be the central theme for the layout for the house. The setting was lovely, Lee thought to herself, and rather surprising considering that the ranch appeared to be smack in the middle of nowhere.

She turned from her perusal of the grounds, then walked back to where her luggage was sitting at the foot of the bed. She reached for the smaller of the two cases to begin her unpacking. "I have a feeling that subtle—and some not so subtle—little clashes between the cowboy and me will become something of the norm before this interview is completed."

Dinner later that evening was simple, or so said Grace. She fixed roast beef, potatoes, peas, homemade rolls, and apple pie, and kept urging the guest to, "Just try a little more, honey," till Lee thought she would explode, and laughingly said so.

"Hmph," Grace snorted. "You girls nowadays don't eat enough to keep a cat alive." She stalked off to the kitchen, grumbling under her breath all the way.

"You'll have to forgive her being so bossy." Ralt laughed. "Being the only woman here has left her with the idea that whoever comes through the front door should automatically do as she decides."

"I don't mind." Lee smiled, then became mortified as she felt a yawn coming on and tried to disguise it! "I'm sorry." She shook her head in embarrassment. "I can't imagine why I'm so sleepy." She glanced down at the slim gold watch on her wrist, and became even more horrified. "It's only seven fifteen."

Ralt grinned, then reached out and caught her hand

in his. "Don't worry, you haven't offended me. The ranch often has that effect on my guests. Especially after one of Grace's huge meals. Her food, combined with the slightly higher elevation and the cool air at night, tends to put one straight to sleep."

Later, she took a seat on a long, comfortable sofa in the large den at the back of the house where the reflection of the moon could be seen in the pool, then accepted a glass of wine from a bottle Ralt told her that he'd been saving for a special occasion.

At one point during the evening Lee found her wineglass empty. At another, she was sprawled rather elegantly—or inelegantly, she couldn't decide which—across Ralt's thighs, her head gently pillowed against his chest. During another spurt of awareness, she heard herself murmuring strange little noises as Ralt's mouth took gentle possession of hers. His lips were gentle but firm in their quest to seek out and capture her response that was already beginning as her lips parted and welcomed him. Sweet, sharp jets of desire fragmented into cascading showers that consumed her body like the ebb and flow of an early-morning tide.

Cool air briefly touched the tips of her breasts, and was quickly replaced by a rough palm that slid warm and protectively from one nipple to another. Long, curling fingers of need began to awaken throughout her body, creating a deep aching in the pit of her stomach. God! She wanted him with such intensity, she felt her body stiffen with the longing.

Ralt felt the slight stiffening and immediately his arms holding her tightened. "Don't pull away from me," he said huskily, his lips moving to her ear, then lower to the rapidly throbbing pulse in the side of her throat.

Lee smiled. The cowboy was so ridiculous. She wasn't pulling away. Couldn't he tell? Couldn't he see? Couldn't he feel the desire-laden weight of her body that was crying out for his care? His loving. "Don't be silly." She smiled at him through the haze of her emotions. "I'm doing everything short of seducing you, and I'm even beginning to think about that. Does that sound like pulling away?"

Ralt was silent for several mind-tingling seconds. His gaze met and made love with hers as surely and passionately as though their bodies were joined. "You've accused me before of telling, not asking. Does that hold true in this instance? Do I have to ask you?" His voice was barely above a whisper, its gravelly quality causing her hand to reach out tremulously and brush the invincible line of his jaw. She loved to hear him talk, for he had an incredibly sexy voice.

"No," she whispered, arching against the hand palming her breast. "There's only one rule."

"Name it," he rushed determinedly.

"No obligations. No strings."

Ralt hesitated. Ordinarily he would have been the one issuing such stipulations. Now, for some unknown reason, he found himself resenting the fact that, here, in the face of sharing something he knew would be beautiful, she could be so callous, so insensitive.

He swallowed his resentment. Claiming Lee as his own was more important than any dent in his pride, he told himself. Changing her mind could come later. At the moment, he wanted nothing more than to drown in the luminous pools of her green eyes, while her body opened to him and absorbed him into her own softness and warmth.

Time was suspended as the discarding of clothes became a slow, exquisitely painful process. Lips found special delight in paying homage to a bared breast, to each wide tanned shoulder or a muscular chest, the concave stomach and gently flared hips. When it was naked skin against naked skin, the friction of rough against soft, of darkly tanned skin against honey-colored skin, each of the senses seemed to take on new meaning, rather than the commonplace functions.

Lee was surprised to find herself totally uninhibited with Ralt. Her only worry was that someone could walk in on them and she mentioned this.

"Don't worry," he murmured against the tiny whorl of her navel, his tongue circling and circling, then dipping in to tease the sensitive center. "Every evening Grace gets to her television as quickly as possible. She's addicted to the damn thing—Which is a blessing." He sighed. "I couldn't control myself if Satan himself were to decide to join us."

He continued the soft caressing of her body with his tongue and lips, his hands stroking, his fingers invading secret places that hadn't known a man's touch for so long. Lee could have sworn she was being flung into a head wind. She felt warm, hot, a faint film of perspiration on her skin; then a second later a cooling shower invaded her senses leaving her icy cold to the touch. Just as she was positive the force of the maelstrom holding her in its grip was pushing her into the

135

softness of the sofa, she felt her hips arching, lifting to the questing tip of the cowboy's tongue.

He touched the inner softness of her femininity. She cried out—a tiny cry of hurting—of loving the hurting, of wanting it to continue, of being afraid of dying if it didn't continue.

He withdrew a fraction of an inch, and she writhed in a moment of confusion, her hands grasping at his head to bring him back to her.

Slowly and deliberately, he stroked her, a hoarse response sounding from him at her aroused cry demanding fulfillment.

With quick, sure movements, Ralt eased his large body over Lee's. He framed her face with his hands as he gently parted her thighs and rested against her for a moment.

"Open your eyes, sweetheart," he whispered hoarsely, forcing himself to wait, to make it as wonderful for her as he knew it was going to be for him.

He was being tested, he told himself. He had to be a better lover than Lance Porter.

Don't be ridiculous, his voice of common sense scolded him. Making love to a beautiful woman isn't something to be approached in a competitive state.

But in Ralt's heart, he knew he was fighting something far greater than simply a woman who had been married before. More and more he was finding that he wanted to be number one in Lee's heart and in her life.

His manhood pressed against the moistness awaiting it. Lee rose to meet the thrust, taking him and encircling that part of him in a narrow, silken cocoon that brought a deep shudder to his muscled frame. The rhythm increased. The thrusts became deeper, the response greater.

He offered, she took. He asked, she nodded and flirted, turning and gesturing for him to follow. The game continued till passion, till flirtations, till emotions were raw and the moment of accounting had arrived.

Ralt felt himself exploding, his arms tightening convulsively around the slight figure he was holding against his chest. Lee heard his harsh cry of release and answered with her own, as the splendor of their climax painted rainbow shades across the midnight sky of her mind.

CHAPTER EIGHT

Lee stood hypnotized! Her body was as unmoving as a post planted in fifty feet of concrete. Her face became a rigid, unreadable mask as she stared at the approaching men and the animals they were leading. The smaller of the two men, she assumed him to be a ranchhand, didn't concern her very much—other than the horse he was leading.

The other man was the same devastating man who had made love to her the night before, but who looked totally different this morning in the roughness of the terrain, dressed in a blue work shirt, faded jeans worn low on his lean hips and scruffy boots. Lee was reminded of the Marlboro commercials. He looked rugged, vital, and completely at peace with his surroundings.

One of the animals was huge. Quite probably the tallest Lee had ever seen. Its large chocolate-colored eyes bore mercilessly into her frightened ones as men and beasts approached her. Lee ran the tip of her tongue over bone-dry lips. "Th-those are horses." The words came out in a peculiar croaking sound, not unlike a giant bullfrog.

"So they are." Ralt nodded, one side of his mouth pulling down as he made a valiant effort not to laugh outright at her inane remark. God! She was the most beautiful thing he'd ever seen, he thought as he watched her. Last night she'd been like quicksilver in his arms. Every inch of her body had filled his hands, then fashioned itself to his form and literally blew the hinges off the windows of his mind.

Suddenly a premonition, as jarring as a bolt of lightning, hit Ralt. He was falling in love with Lee Cantrell, a woman he'd known only a short while, but one he felt he'd known all his life. He wanted— No, he quickly corrected himself. He *would* have her in his future.

He and his entourage paused three or four feet away. The shy, young ranchhand ducked his blond head, his hat shielding his features.

"Horses," Lee said again, as though repeating the word might possibly have some slight significance on the outcome of what she knew was going to be a disastrous event.

She could never remember a time she wasn't afraid of horses, cows, pigs and all the other critters that made up the usual conglomeration seen in children's books. Her recollections of visits to an uncle's farm were the pits. She was a city girl, she often told herself, so why should she have cultivated a relationship with any of the four-footed friends? Dogs and cats were different. She would like to own one of each, but living in apartments prevented her from that small enjoyment.

Ralt looked at her out of the corner of his eye. His

139

favorite old, worn cowboy hat was pulled low over his forehead. Lee could barely see his eyes, but she knew by the set of his shoulders and the peculiar little catch in his rusty voice that he was laughing at her. She knew darned well his hired help was laughing as well.

"Yes, ma'am." Ralt nodded solemnly. "Two genuine horses. A mare," he slapped the auburn-haired beauty nearest him affectionately on the rump, and continued to caress the satiny neck beneath the thick mane, "and a stallion," indicating the midnight-black animal pawing at the ground with one front hoof. "Horses remind me of women, they like to know who's master. Then as long as they're worked hard, fed well, and have a clean, dry place to sleep, they're happy as pigs in the sunshine." He kept darting short, laugh-filled glances at his guest. "Yessiree, these are horses. Four legs, a head, long tail and a mane. All those things add up to a horse."

"Please forgive me," Lee cooed sweetly. "In my natural stupidity regarding such things, I naturally assumed those things added up to one huge ass."

The ranchhand made a noise that sounded as if he'd swallowed something the wrong way. He turned his back on his boss and the reporter lady from New Orleans.

Ralt wasn't amused. He wasn't accustomed to a woman putting him down in front of his men, at the ranch or in the office.

Lee jammed her hands on her hips and glared at him. "Are these horses the reason you had Grace wake me up before daylight?"

"Six o'clock is a perfectly reasonable hour, Ms. Cantrell."

"Really?"

"Hell, yes. I assumed you'd enjoy a nice ride before breakfast."

"Then you've started off your day by making one whopping big mistake, haven't you?" she practically hissed. How dare he! How dare he!

"What the hell is that supposed to mean?" Ralt glared. At first he'd been amused by her apprehension. Now he felt more like turning her across his lap and paddling her cute little behind. Was she deliberately trying to sabotage their time together?

"Just because you live on a ranch, cowboy, and ride those pesky things," she pointed one long, oval-tipped finger toward the horses, "doesn't mean the whole damned world is clamoring to try the same thing. I drink milk, but I sure as hell don't want to go visit the cow it came from. I enjoy bacon and eggs for breakfast, but I certainly don't want a pig or rooster on my patio. Now do you understand?"

"A rooster won't give you eggs, Ms. Cantrell."

"What?"

"You said 'a pig and rooster on your patio.' Hens lay eggs. Roosters just strut around the hen house keeping the ladies happy." He turned to a vastly amused cowhand. "Thanks, Hap. By the way." He nodded curtly toward Lee. "This is Hap Davis. He's one of my top hands on the ranch."

After a few stilted words of conversation fraught with Lee's anxiety, Hap walked back to the barn, and Lee resumed her address.

141

"I suppose you were planning on me riding that
. . . that monster." With an angry nod of her head,
she indicated the stallion.

"Certainly," Ralt rounded with a straight face. "I'd
planned on strapping you in the saddle and sticking a
cattle prod to old Satan here. Little form of western
hospitality we reserve for special guests."

"This is a ridiculous conversation." She turned on
her heel, but before she could take a single step, she
felt a grip of iron on her upper arm, then felt herself
being swung back around.

Ralt was angry. "You are going riding with me.
Now. This morning. Understand?" His gaze bore into
hers, daring her to disagree with him.

Not adverse to switching tack when faced with certain insurmountable obstacles, Lee chewed nervously
at her bottom lip. "Please, McLean. Animals make me
nervous. I only like cats and dogs. I'm a city girl. Remember?"

"I'll be right beside you all the way, Lee," he said
gruffly. There was magic in his hands as they gently
smoothed their way up and down her arms. "Do you
honestly think I'd let you try anything that would
harm you in any way?" His gaze caressed her with its
warmth, and brought a profusion of pink to her cheeks
as vivid scenes from the evening before floated in and
out of her mind.

"Well . . . no . . ." she said slowly. "I don't suppose you would."

"Thank you." Ralt tipped his dark head slightly, his
mouth caught in a mocking twist. "You should be
careful, honey. Such expressions of trust might turn

142

my head." All the while he spoke, he was leading her around to the left side of the mare. "Now this little lady is called Sweetpea. She's gentle as a lamb."

Lee took a deep breath, eyeing Sweetpea with about as much pleasure as one would the guillotine. Sweetpea retaliated in kind, even to turning her head and watching Lee.

One minute Lee was listening intently to Ralt explain the intricacies of getting into the saddle, and the next minute Sweetpea found the most inviting spot on Lee's fanny and bit down.

"Ouch!" Lee yelled in a voice that quickly brought several interested heads to the door of the sprawling barn. The hands had never seen the Boss handle a woman such as Miz Cantrell. It was proving to be quite a show. "That damned horse just bit me." Lee glared accusingly at Ralt and the mare as she rubbed both hands against that part of her anatomy that was now smarting. "McLean," she said murderously, "I refuse to ride any beast that bites me."

Ralt didn't answer.

Lee peered closer at him. Why was he holding his head in that peculiar one-sided way? Was he listening for something?

"Damn you, McLean! Did you hear me?"

She saw his shoulders shake—only a little bit at first, but they definitely shook. There. There it was again. Why he was laughing at her, Lee fumed. The great huge ass was laughing at her, because his dumb horse had bitten her.

Lee gathered together what was left of her dignity,

threw her host a withering look, then walked back to the house, through the back door and into the kitchen.

"Back so soon?" Grace looked up from removing long crisp slices of bacon out of a huge iron skillet.

"I didn't go anywhere," Lee informed her coolly. "I won't be eating breakfast, Grace. I'd appreciate it if you'd see about having Raz or one of the hands take me into town in about thirty minutes."

"Into town?" Grace frowned. "What on earth for?"

"Because I'll be returning to New Orleans today."

"But I thought you were going to do an interview on the boss?"

"And so I was," Lee said thoughtfully, keeping a firm hold on her temper, which was seething just below the surface. "However, the more I think about it, and the more I see of your boss, I'm convinced someone else should do the job. I don't like horses, I don't like cows, and I sure as hell don't like the country."

"Oh, my," Grace murmured, shaking her gray head, her mouth glued in a perpetual "O" shape. "Does Ralt know how you feel?"

"I suspect by now he's gotten the picture," Lee replied. "I'd appreciate it if you'd see about that ride for me, Grace. I promise to be ready in thirty minutes."

"Forget about any ride, Gracie," Ralt said from the doorway. "Ms. Cantrell won't be leaving after all."

Lee swung around at the first sound of his voice, her small body quivering with rage. "You haven't the slightest say in when I go or come, Ralt McLean. I—"

She was interrupted by Ralt calmly walking over, picking her up in his arms and striding out of the kitchen. His, "I don't know how you handle it in New

Orleans, but here in Texas, we don't discuss all our business in public. We save some things for the bedroom."

When he reached the guest room Lee was using, he walked inside, then caught the door with the tip of his boot and slammed it. Instead of putting Lee down, as she was continuously instructing him in a loud voice to do, he didn't stop till he was beside the bed where he dropped her in an angry heap.

The moment she hit the mattress, Lee began scrambling to the other side and safety.

Ralt was faster. He caught one slender ankle and slowly pulled her toward him. With all the scrambling around she was doing, her shirt was completely out of her jeans. Now, as her body slid against the spread, her shirttail hitched higher and higher, revealing more and more of her honey-colored skin and the beginnings of her small firm breasts.

Just as the beginnings of the pinkish areola around the nipple began to play a provocative game of hide-and-seek with Ralt, he stopped. He came down swiftly over Lee, one large hand splayed—palm down—on one side of her face, while the other one found its way to her breasts.

His breath was sweet on her face, and the scent of him smelled like the freshness of the outdoors. If he'd been a gentleman he would have stayed across the room—at least until the quarrel was over with.

"I'm not about to let you leave me, Lee. Don't you realize that?"

How was it possible for him to do such beautifully sensitive things to her body? How was it possible for her to almost hate him one minute, yet the next allow herself to be drawn into that special plane of awareness that only he awakened in her?

"You make it sound like a threat, McLean," she said in a breathless voice.

"It is. If you leave me, I'll take out ads in all the papers in Texas and Louisiana. I'll say you came into my home, that you let me make love to you, that you cast a spell over me, and then threw me aside—all for the sake of one lousy interview." His gaze fairly sparkled with amusement and desire as he stared down into her face and then lower—to the perfect pink nipple to which he was paying such minute attention. Yet in spite of all his attempts at playing the comedian, Lee also saw the seriousness in his eyes and it bothered her.

"That's a crock, McLean, and you know it." She tried to sound stern, trying with all her might to summon the anger she'd felt only moments ago. "But even if you did, I'd be forced to tell my side of the story as well. Interesting copy, hmm? When I got through, you'd have every female reporter in the world out in your front yard wanting a sample of your Texas hospitality. The kind you shared with me last night, not the horse- and cattle-prod variety."

Ralt grinned down at her. "You're a mean-hearted little witch."

Lee saw him coming closer and tried to prepare herself for the onslaught of his kiss. But as with everything else where he was concerned, she had very little control over the situation or her response. Her mouth received his eagerly just as her arms encircled his neck

146

and her body arched to meet the incredibly potent feel of him. His touch was warm, and gentle, and rough and cool. In the fragments of her mind, Lee wondered how all those feelings were possible in one instance when they were so contradictory.

With a deep rush of air bursting from his lungs, Ralt suddenly released Lee and rolled over onto his back. He ran a hand over his face before turning and staring at the woman beside him, her face flushed, her lips still parted and moist from his kiss.

He gently touched his thumb to her upper lip and rubbed it back and forth. He explored further, moving inside her bottom lip and the edges of her teeth. Lee allowed her tongue to sheath his thumb, then began nibbling it. Ralt turned on his side and watched her intently through shuttered lids. The sensations caused by her mouth were arousing him as deeply as if their bodies were intimately joined.

"Do you do it deliberately?" he whispered huskily. He leaned forward and caught the tip of her ear between his lips. Lee turned into his embrace, her body warm and throbbing, the proof of his arousal pressed tightly against her belly.

"Do what?" she whispered.

"Excite me . . . make me want to do all sorts of extremely wicked things to you. To put it bluntly, Ms. Cantrell, you turn me on. You keep me in a constant state of wanting to be in bed with you, actually being there and/or thinking of ways of accomplishing that fact."

"Mmm . . . You make me feel positively wanton, cowboy." She teased him with her fingers slowly moving along the buttons of his shirt, from time to time slipping inside to caress his chest. With the tip of her tongue, she concentrated on memorizing the sensuous outline of his mouth. Even her eyes were issuing an openly provocative message, flirting with his, daring him to come after her.

"If I arrange my schedule so that I'm in New Orleans more, will you move in with me?"

Lee blinked her eyes as if to clear them. She honestly wasn't that surprised by the suggestion, but at that precise moment, it was unexpected. "Thank you, but I'm not in the market for a roommate."

Suddenly she could feel resentment for him creeping into their midst. He was tampering with her life, and she didn't like that at all. Certainly, she told herself, making love with him the night before had been the most wonderful thing she'd ever experienced. But moving in with him. Well, Lee reasoned, that smacked of commitment. She hadn't fared too well in the commitment department with Lance, and nothing had happened since that disastrous failure to make her think she was any more capable now of handling a special relationship than she was then.

His displeasure to her response was reflected in Ralt's eyes; by their swift change from the azure hue intensified with passion, to ice blue. As Lee watched, she was shocked at how quickly they could change.

"The relationship I have in mind would be a bit more sophisticated than a mere roommate, Lee," he said bluntly. "I'm . . . interested in you. More so than any woman I've ever known. At the moment I'm incapable of getting a clear grasp on the reasons you intrigue me, but suffice it to say you do."

"When you're angry, which you are right now," Lee pointed out gently as her forefinger lightly sketched the slant of each of his brows, "you sound like a pompous ass." She was buying time, she silently argued. Buying time by trying to reason with him. At the moment, her feelings for him were a jumbled mess. He fascinated her. He made beautiful things happen to her body. She enjoyed being with him. His touch, his gaze, his voice, each of these things about him, was capable of flooding her body with desire. Being with him was comparable to riding on a supercharged merry-go-round. Only problem was, Lee knew the time would come when the merry-go-round would stop, the music would slowly fade, and cold reality would replace the euphoria.

Ralt caught her wrist and imprisoned her hand against his chest, the steady beat of his heart against her skin a pleasant sensation. It was strong and vital, the same as McLean. "Pompous ass or not, you haven't answered my question. Will you move in with me? There'll be no ties, no restrictions. If one of us wishes to sever the relationship at any time, the other must respect those wishes."

Lee smiled. She leaned forward and kissed the stern mouth, finding it strangely disconcerting to be offering comfort, of a sort, to this dour-faced man whose wealth and power were awesome.

"No."

Ralt dropped onto his back, a frown creasing his brow. "I wonder what it is you're afraid of?" He knew the same moment of panic he'd experienced when they'd discussed Lance Porter. Lee denied still being in love with her ex-husband, but was she being one hundred percent truthful?

"Why do I have to be afraid of something? Why can't it be you that's got some sort of hang-up?"

"I haven't the slightest problem admitting that I'm definitely not interested in marriage and that I enjoy the company of beautiful women—till recently—when one beautiful woman in particular caught my attention. I'm sure there are other things in my makeup that someone might find strange, but for the most part I think I'm fairly normal." He watched her closely. "Since we seem to be sharing our deep, dark secrets, do you care to explain this uneasiness I've sensed in you the few times there's been any mention of our relationship becoming more personal?"

"Why are you so opposed to marriage?" Lee countered.

"Wasn't there an account of Sally's death in any of those files you studied so diligently?" he asked coolly.

She shook her head, wondering why the question brought such an abrupt change in him. "None that I remember."

"We tried to keep it quiet." He shrugged. "Perhaps we were more successful than I thought." He raised his arms and crossed them behind his head, his gaze trained on the delicate stitchery of the canopy that sheltered the antique bed. "Sally was kidnapped from a department store in Dallas, and held for ransom. There's no way I can explain the fear Douglas Nelson and I lived through during that time. After much dealing with the kidnappers, which the authorities were in on, we paid the ransom. The fact that the authorities were involved hadn't surfaced, and everything was going relatively well till somehow a smart-ass reporter got wind of the negotiations and thought it would make great copy. He talked his editor into printing the story, using the wornout cry that 'the public has a right to know.' Well the public found out. And the kidnappers found out—and Sally's body was found twenty-four hours later. She'd been choked to death."

Lee lay in stunned disbelief. No wonder he was so cynical. "I'm sorry," she whispered. "I really am."

Ralt turned his dark head and smiled gruffly at her. "I know. But I'm over Sally's death now, Lee. So don't start thinking I'm carrying a torch for her. I'm not."

"And that's why you have such a strong dislike for reporters?"

"Precisely. That's also why I promised never to marry again. No woman deserves to be put in that position. Don't you think I'm justified?"

"I suppose you are," she said slowly. "Yet I know any number of reporters who wouldn't dream of doing something so underhanded. I honestly hate to see you condemn all of us just because you were unfortunate enough to have a dreadful experience with one lowlife."

In a quick, fluid move, Ralt reached for her and pulled her on top of him. "I don't dislike all reporters, honey." His hands slipped beneath her shirt and began smoothing their way up and down her back, dipping to the sides of her rib cage and brushing against the flattened softness of her breast. "In fact, there's one I'm

151

particularly fond of, and I can't wait to see her on a horse."

He grinned evilly, and Lee dipped her head and bit him on the tip of his ear. His yelp of pain brought a smile of pure pleasure to her face. "Did that hurt?" she asked sweetly.

"Hell yes." Ralt scowled, although his hands hadn't lessened their caresses in the least.

"Good. Let that be a reminder to you that I do not ride horses, I do not like cows, and I do not care for the wide-open spaces."

"Really? Is that a challenge?" Ralt grinned.

"Certainly not. It's a statement of fact."

"You're telling me that you positively will not ride a horse?"

"Positively."

"Ms. Cantrell, darling, I sure as hell hope you brought plenty of liniment for aching muscles. For a novice, riding can be quite painful."

"All I have to say to that is, the novice is a fool for getting astride the horse."

Two hours later, Lee's eyes were glazed over with a peculiar expression of pain, disbelief, and the realization of a distinct prickly numbness in certain areas of her body.

She remembered swearing in a loud voice. Loud enough to bring half the hands to the corral fence to see the show. She distinctly remembered having sworn to have a contract put out on McLean's despicable head, but that threat hadn't slowed him in the least from placing her firmly in the saddle, thrusting her feet into the stirrups and then forcing the reins into her hands.

From that point, they'd begun what was, without a doubt, the most god-awful experience of Lee's life, or so she kept telling herself as she hung on to the reins, the saddle horn and even the mare's mane a couple of times. Each command she gave the mare, at Ralt's suggestion, was totally ignored by Sweetpea.

When Lee loosened her death grip on the reins and touched her heels to the auburn flanks, Sweetpea looked around as if she couldn't believe her eyes. A quick slap on the rear from Ralt sent horse and rider off into the sunset. As the journey progressed, Lee's cries of "Whoa!" were met with total disregard. Only when Sweetpea wanted to stop for a snack along the way did the wild foray come to a halt, further humiliating Lee and causing her to curse herself for ever agreeing to interview Ralt McLean in the first place.

Their inauspicious arrival back at the ranch saw a grim-faced Lee slip from the saddle, her legs resembling stiff poles. She grasped at Ralt's shoulders for support, knowing that if she didn't, she would fall flat on her behind.

He took her weight against his body, his arms drawing her close to him. "I know you had some problems," he said against her hair, "but didn't you really enjoy it? Wasn't it fantastic feeling the wind through your hair . . . against your face?"

Lee drew back enough to glare at him. "Watch my lips, cowboy. I did not enjoy it! There was no wind blowing through my hair or in my face, and that fat horse," nodding toward the unconcerned Sweetpea,

153

"is no pleasure to ride." With all her heart, she wanted to spin around on her heel and walk haughtily away. However, she reasoned, what with her legs practically immovable and her rear end needing a hot soak, a thorough rubdown and quite probably a shot of Novocain, she had no choice but to ask for McLean's assistance to the house.

"After a hot bath you'll be ready to go again," he remarked innocently as he guided her down the hallway to her room. It took some doing on Ralt's part to ignore the murderous look shot his way. "By the way, I've called a meeting this evening with Josh Emmett and some of the ranchers to discuss the illegal alien situation. Care to come with me?"

Lee perked up at the invitation. The meeting, and the reason it was being called, could work up into an entirely different story. "Will you be driving a motored vehicle or riding a damned horse?" she asked nastily.

CHAPTER NINE

The room was large, and through a door on the right, Lee caught a glimpse of a fully equipped kitchen. From all appearances it seemed this must be the meeting place for just about every function held in the small town of Domingo.

She looked at the faces of the men, and a few women who had chosen to attend, most already seated at a long table at the opposite end of the room. She noted the grim-jawed determination marking each man's features. Their faces were tanned and leathery, with tiny wrinkles snaking out from the corners of their eyes—apparently brought on from years of squinting against the brightness of the sun.

They looked to be tough and hard working, and Lee felt herself warming to the lot of them. One in particular had her laughing practically the moment she stepped inside the meeting room.

"My name is Steve Crandall." The tall, blond cowboy blocked her way. There was a gleam of mischief in his blue eyes that caused Lee to almost shake her head outright. He stuck out his hand, his grasp as strong as Ralt's. "That miserly McLean and I are neighbors.

155

You'd think he'd invite me over to meet his beautiful house guest, wouldn't you? But I haven't heard a single word from him since you arrived. Can you beat that?"

"Simply terrible." Lee laughed as she introduced herself.

"Don't listen to a thing this fellow tells you, honey," Ralt said as he quickly materialized between Lee and Steven. He slipped an arm around her waist and caught her to him. "Fathers in this part of Texas sleep with one eye on their daughters, one on Crandall, and their hand on their shotgun. No female is safe around him."

"Now, honey," said Steven, ignoring Ralt. "Don't pay any attention to McLean. He's jealous of me. I'm much better-looking than him, and he knows it. I don't have quite as much money, but I'm working real hard to catch up. Now if you don't mind waiting for a few months, I'll be able to entertain you in the same grand style I'm certain he's promised you."

"Thank you, Steven." Lee chuckled. "It helps knowing I have a choice. Just one thing, though. Do you require your guests to ride?"

"Certainly not," he quipped. "I've never cared for the sport myself."

"And a bigger lie I've yet to hear," Ralt scoffed. "What this no-good isn't telling you is that he spends a good part of each year on the rodeo circuit."

"A punishment," Steven waved one hand grandly, "a mere punishment. If I had you, I'd be content to stay on the ranch forever."

"That would be terrible," Lee remarked with mock seriousness.

"Keep talking, Crandall," Ralt said silkily, "you're doing real good."

"Did I detect some faint hostility directed toward ranching?" Steve's wicked glance danced back and forth between Lee and Ralt.

"I don't know about the faintness," Ralt informed him, "but there are those of us, and I refuse to name names, who are diametrically opposed to any sort of existence other than the concrete one within some large metropolis."

Steven looked down at Lee and grinned. "Then it most certainly is my duty to show those of us who feel this way how wrong they are, and how delightful the western way of life can be."

"Your generosity overwhelms me." Ralt stared grimly at him. His arm around Lee's waist tightened. "You can be assured I'll take care of any convincing that needs doing." The silly arguing continued till Ralt left Lee and Steven at their seats, then went to the front of the room and called the meeting to order.

It quickly became obvious that, for the most part, Ralt's fellow ranchers were just as concerned with the alien problem as he was. However, there were two or three who were quite apprehensive because of what had happened in the past.

"It's not that I don't see the need, Ralt," one man spoke up. "I just can't forget about what happened to Sam Hayman. You had a mighty bad fire at your place as well."

"That's true, John." Ralt nodded, and Lee felt a

157

rush of pleasure as she listened to him commiserate with John regarding the man's fears, then slowly bring him around to Ralt's way of thinking.

During the course of the meeting others had specific ideas or opinions on the subject, some favorable, some not. Ralt listened, added a thought or comment at times, then shared his views. Lee was amazed at how easily he handled the men, though what impressed her most of all was the fact that the others were ranchers —just the same as Ralt. They all owned large spreads, ran large herds, and had various other interests. He wasn't the oldest nor the youngest, but there was a definite air of leadership about him that caught and held the attention of his neighbors.

The meeting lasted well over two hours, and during that time plans were made, meeting dates set, and a liaison between the authorities and the ranchers chosen. The rash of rustling that was plaguing most everyone present was discussed. Most were convinced that particular crime was separate from the illegal aliens. A few thought otherwise.

Lee was curious as to Ralt's opinion, and asked him about it on the way home.

"Frankly I think the two are entirely separate crimes, but possibly run by the same great minds. On the other hand, there could be no connection other than the rustlers somehow coordinating their visits to our ranches about the same time there's a sizable group crossing the river."

"How do you feel about trying to keep the authorities happy and satisfy your neighbors? Will that be a problem for you?"

"It shouldn't. Most of the ranchers are fairly level-headed. Right now they're uptight over the situation. What didn't come out at the meeting was the fact that two or three have aliens working for them. Cheap labor's hard to come by. Any way you look at it, it's a touchy situation."

Lee was quiet for a moment. "Someone mentioned Sam Hayman. Who is he?"

"Sam was a neighbor. He and I tried this same thing a while back. One night Sam was coming home from a meeting. He got out of his car, took two steps, and was shot three times in the back. That same night, my barn, holding several fine horses, was burned to the ground. The fire was started in such a manner as to engulf the outer perimeter of the building and it was impossible to reach the animals."

Lee felt the cold hand of fear clutching her heart as it dawned on her just how dangerous the situation really was. "You must feel very strongly about the subject."

Ralt nodded, his gaze never leaving the road. "I do. I feel sorry for those people trying to get into this country. They're pathetic. Yet there is a right and a wrong way in which to become a citizen. One has to look at all sides of the problem, honey. People from other countries have to obey immigration laws and rules . . . for the most part. Why not the Mexicans? Then there's the scum that makes money on the poor wretches by promising to have a job waiting for them and to get them across without being apprehended. It's a damned series of indignities mankind heaps upon mankind—leaving people like us, the observers so to

159

speak, to wonder to what level man will sink in order to grasp wealth."

Lee shivered. "Put like that, it makes the human race look pretty bad."

A cold, humorless laugh escaped Ralt. "The human race *is* pretty bad, honey. Certain segments of my life reflect how low we humans can sink."

For the remainder of the time it took them to get back to the ranch, Lee was quiet. She was concerned for the tall, rangy man beside her. That fact alone stood out above all else. The thought of the same thing happening to him that had befallen Sam Hayman preyed heavily on her mind.

"You're awfully quiet," Ralt said huskily as he opened the car door for her. "Something troubling you?"

"Oh . . ." Lee fumbled around for something to say, thankful the darkness concealed her guilty expression, "I was just thinking of the meeting, and what an interesting story it will make."

"Ahh yes." He exhaled noisily. "We mustn't forget the reason you're here, must we?" He caught her elbow and escorted her into the house. "When are you going to break out the tape recorder and begin asking your questions?"

"Actually, I hadn't planned on conducting the interview quite like that. I prefer the more casual approach," Lee said briskly, wondering what had happened to set him off. She looked up at him. His jaw was clenched, and his lips were a rigid line of disapproval. Okay, she told herself, so he's ticked off about something. Fine. Everybody was entitled once in a while, but he could damned sure take it out on some-one else. She wasn't about to be his personal goat.

"Good night, McLean." Without touching him, she turned and walked away.

Ralt watched her leave him, his eyes running over the soft outline of her body. All right, you sap, he began lecturing himself, you're in love with her, aren't you? You've gone and allowed the worst possible thing to happen. The one thing that can destroy both of you. It's totally stupid. Can't you see that?

He strode down the hall opposite the one Lee had taken, till he came to the large den at the back of the house. Once there, he went straight to the liquor cabi-net. He hooked two fingers around the neck of a bottle of Chivas Regal, reached for a glass with the other hand, then headed for a redwood lounger beside the pool.

He splashed a generous portion of Scotch into the glass, then settled back against the cushion, memories from the past pushing into his mind. Memories of Sally and her kidnapping, and thoughts of how easily it could happen again . . . to Lee.

As the minutes stretched into hours, Ralt felt the most god-awful aching in his chest. At certain mo-ments he was positive his heart was going to explode. He loved Lee—loved her with a desperation that was numbing. Yet he knew he would have to let her go. The meeting and seeing the fear in his neighbors' faces had brought back painful memories. And even though Sally's death hadn't been related to the current prob-lems the ranchers were experiencing, it only took one sick mind to repeat the tragedy.

161

A deep, agonizing burst of air rushed from Ralt's chest as he stared at the velvet sky through eyes misted with tears. He thought he'd been given his chance—the chance to marry the woman he loved—to have babies with her. But it wasn't to be, and all his wealth couldn't change that. He was destined to remain in that nether world of loneliness, a prisoner of his own success and the sickness of society.

Before she went to bed, Lee moved over to the French doors and stared out at the pool and the moonlight reflected there. It took a moment or two for her to notice the quiet, still figure on the lounger. Without thinking, her hand went to the doorknob. He needed her.

He was hurting inside. Lee knew it as surely as she knew the pain in her own heart. Seeing him in such despair tore her apart—she wanted to take him in her arms and tell him that she loved him.

She became rigid. Apprehension in each line of her slight body.

Love.

She loved the cowboy?

Certainly not, she hastily corrected herself. She wasn't ready for that sort of confusion in her life. Hadn't she thought the same thing once before? Besides, she needed to get on with her career. If she did a good enough story on McLean, Cole would continue to give her bigger and better assignments. Assignments that would lead to other, more prominent publications. Perhaps, in a few years, even television.

She released her tight grip on the doorknob. No, she tried to convince herself, now wasn't the time to try to comfort McLean. She couldn't let him see the depth of her emotions, which was too easily read in her face. Besides, they were both loners, accustomed to sorting out their problems alone.

The cowboy needed space, and so did she. But Lee continued to watch the solitary figure. Eventually, tears glimmered like freshly spun silken threads on Lee's cheeks. Her heart told her they needed each other, but her common sense told her it would only lead to further heartache. Finally she turned from her silent, lonely vigil and made her way to the bed.

Inside she felt as if she were dying with loneliness.

The next morning Lee paused in the doorway of the large, comfortable kitchen to find Ralt reading the *Wall Street Journal* while he sipped a cup of coffee. She somehow managed to walk—without screaming—to the table, in her mind damning all horses to hell and back.

Ralt rose to his feet and pulled out her chair for her. "Good morning, sleepyhead." His bold blue eyes embraced her, caressed each dip and curve of her body, then lingered on her mouth.

Lee could feel the heat of a blush stealing over her face. No man had ever made love to her with his eyes. It was a heady experience.

"Good morning," she managed as she carefully allowed her rear end to make contact with the chair. From what she could see, he looked none the worse for having spent a number of hours in the company of a bottle of Scotch. Was he in any better mood than he'd been the evening before?

The longer Ralt stared at Lee, the more he began

163

doubting the decision he'd reached the evening before. Could he really go through with it?

Grace bustled over with a steaming cup of coffee and a plate heaped with scrambled eggs, ham, and hash brown potatoes. "You'll find hot biscuits there." She nodded toward a small round basket, covered by a red and white checked napkin. "I was beginning to think you were ill or something."

Lee glanced down at her watch, then back to the housekeeper. "But it's just barely seven o'clock."

"I know." Grace nodded. "Your breakfast has been ready since six thirty. I assumed you'd be going riding with Ralt."

"Er, Lee isn't into riding just yet, Gracie," Ralt spoke up.

The older woman jammed a fist on her hip and openly regarded Lee. "You didn't enjoy riding yesterday?" she asked incredulously.

"No," Lee said flatly. "Is that some sort of crime?"

Grace appeared baffled. "I suppose not. What will you do when you and Ralt marry? I mean, every year he hosts a huge barbecue here at the ranch. Among the festivities there are always two or three riding events for the ladies. Are you going to allow that silly Carrie Warren to take your place?"

"Well, I mean, I'm not," Lee stammered.

Ralt rested his forehead against the tips of his fingers and briefly closed his eyes. One day soon, he promised himself, he was going to have Grace's mouth permanently sutured closed. "Grace," he said stiffly. "I'd like more coffee please—now."

"Nonsense. I just poured you a refill," Grace an-

164

swered matter-of-factly, not even bothering to glance his way. "Now you listen to me, honey." She directed her full attention to Lee. "Don't let some silly disagreement keep you from enjoying your stay here. You'll be much happier after you and Ralt are married, if you share all of his life."

"McLean and I are not getting married, Grace," Lee said distinctly.

"Certainly you are." Grace nodded. "Raz and I discussed it. We think you'll make the perfect wife for the Boss." She fondly regarded the two seated at the table for several seconds, then turned and walked to the stove, humming happily.

Lee turned from watching Grace, her expression bewildered, to face Ralt. "She's *your* housekeeper," she hissed. "Can't you do something with her?"

Ralt shrugged, his annoyance with Grace fading as he watched Lee squirm. "She's getting on in years, you know."

"Getting on in years, my foot!" Lee spluttered. "You encouraged her."

"Me?" he exclaimed innocently. "I didn't say a word."

"My point exactly," Lee swiftly countered. "You—"

"Don't." He leaned forward, the fingers of one large hand touching her lips and staying the angry spate. He smiled then, and Lee felt her heart do a complete flip-flop at the gentleness she saw there. "Let's not start the day arguing."

"But—"

"Why don't you let Grace show you around? You

were so busy yesterday you didn't see much of the place."

"Oh, I was busy all right," she grumbled. "Busy being jostled over rocks and dust till my brain rattled." She paused, wondering why he couldn't show her around. "Are you going to be busy for the day?"

"We lost several head of cattle last night. Raz found some tracks, so I'll be tied up for a few hours."

"I'm beginning to think the illegal aliens and the rustling are one and the same."

"There's not just one person responsible for the border situation, honey," Ralt explained. "I'm sure there are many. One of them could be behind the rustling—who knows?"

"Can't the sheriff take care of it?" All she could think of was him sprawled somewhere in a pool of blood . . . dead from some sniper's bullet. "Please be careful, McLean."

He caught her hand then, and held it tightly. In her eyes he saw concern, and his heart was warmed by it. He thought of the time when she would be gone and he would be back playing the role of the high-powered executive. Two separate lives, two frightened people whose pasts kept them prisoners. He'd made his decision the evening before, he was determined to stick with it. "Don't worry, I'll be all right."

The words of advice were easily given, but they failed to bring an ounce of comfort to Lee as the day wore on and she gingerly followed Grace through the lovely house and the grounds surrounding it. By mid-afternoon, she was aching from her waist to her knees.

Grace caught her wincing as she stepped onto the

concrete apron surrounding the pool. "Still smarting from the ride yesterday?"

"And how. I must have pulled muscles I didn't even know I had." Lee smiled ruefully.

"A good hot soak is about the only thing that will take the soreness away," the housekeeper advised. "That and continuing to ride."

That advice was followed that afternoon, and for the next several days. Lee was tickled pink when she actually saddled the infamous Sweetpea without Ralt's assistance. Though she wasn't as graceful in the saddle as she would have preferred, she was becoming more confident each time out.

She and Ralt rode for miles—in the morning and in the early evening. They talked about the illegal alien project he was working on, they discussed food preferences, books, and political persuasions. Ralt was a Republican, Lee a staunch Democrat. About the only subject not discussed was Lee and her relationship with Lance.

Lee found herself reluctant to try to explain. Ralt was afraid if he pushed, he'd find she still loved Lance Porter. He decided he'd rather think she cared for him than to know she still loved her ex-husband.

Time passed as effortlessly as a gently flowing stream. In the small hours of the night, they made love and Lee knew her heart would remain on the ranch in the Texas hill country, no matter how far away she roamed. She was becoming more and more depressed as the end of her visit loomed closer. For days now, she'd had enough material on Ralt McLean to write ten articles.

So where, she quietly mused late one evening as she stepped from the shower before going to bed, was the sense of accomplishment she should be feeling? And where was some appropriate remedy that would take away the aching in her heart? When was she going to get up enough nerve to say her job was finished?

The soft folds of the huge bath towel swathed her small body from head to foot. She opened the door and entered the connecting bedroom, then came to an abrupt halt.

Ralt was stretched out on her bed, his arms behind his head, his shoulders resting against the sturdy headboard. He wore only a pair of faded jeans, and Lee knew she'd never seen a more sensually exciting picture in her entire life.

"Taking to straying into women's bedrooms, cowboy?" she gently teased as she walked slowly, boldly, over to stand beside the bed and look down at him.

God! He reminded her of the stallion he rode. Savagery, strength, gentleness, and kindness. All those emotions had somehow become intertwined into a mighty surge of power that produced the entity called Ralt McLean. His face was one that caught and held another's attention, his body conveyed a harmonious union, each part flowing effortlessly into the other, merging into one forceful element of strength and beauty.

Rather than a reply, Ralt extended his hand, palm up. Trustingly, Lee put hers in it and felt the fingers close about her slender ones. Her hand holding the towel at her breasts loosened. The soft heavy material slowly eased down her body, inch by inch baring her nakedness. When it was ended, she stood naked before him, a small, spirited goddess, her glowing green eyes peering into his soul and his heart and capturing both.

Ralt swung his feet to the floor and removed his clothing. He swung Lee off her feet and into his arms, then settled back on the bed, holding her thigh to thigh, breast to breast in place on top of him.

Hot, sensitive nipples nestled in his dark chest hair, heated skin embraced heated skin, and callused palms smoothed and punished the impudent thrust of buttocks and the long, slender line of back and shoulders.

Blue gaze merged with green. Each intimate foray mirrored the depth of feeling in those blue and green eyes. Mouths possessed, lips touched and shaped, while tongues teased and savored the taste.

The movements became more hurried, then frenzied, the needs sky-rocketing. Each tried to shut out the inevitable moment when past hurts, past mistakes, and their individual fears of the future would separate them. Each was caught up in their own personal torment, yet intent on giving to the other the total of themselves.

When Ralt claimed Lee in the final and ultimate gift of man to woman, a sharp cry burst from her lips. Tears ran unheeded down her face as she refused to close her eyes, but held his gaze as completely as she was holding him inside her. What Ralt saw rocked him to his very soul, leaving him confused and torn apart with indecision.

He wanted to tell her what was in his heart . . .

tell her that he loved her and wanted to spend the rest
of his life with her. But caution held him back. Caution and the underlying fear that some kind of harm
would come to her because of him.

CHAPTER TEN

Ralt awakened with a totally depressed feeling.

She was leaving after lunch. This was his last morning with Lee. Last night they'd made love with such intensity, such meaning, it had been hours afterward before he'd slept.

Without allowing himself time to dwell on the inevitable, Ralt swung his legs to the floor and stood, just as there was a discreet knock on his door.

"Yes, Grace?"

"It's Raz, Boss."

At Ralt's bid to enter, the foreman opened the door, his expression grim. "Got some bad news." He closed the door and walked on into the room.

Ralt reached for his jeans and stepped into them. "Let's have it."

"I found this tacked to the front door a few minutes ago." He handed Ralt a piece of roughly torn paper. "Damned fellow that left it there must have had wings on his feet."

Ralt read the brief message, his chest tightening as the cold, brutal words sank in. Unless he wanted some accident to befall Lee and Grace, he would halt all

171

involvement in the illegal alien situation, and not worry about losing a few head of cattle now and then. He was told that considering his wealth, he shouldn't mind sharing with his neighbors.

Anger stiffened Ralt's lips. Some lowlife, some bastard, was trying to control his life! "Get hold of the sheriff, Raz. Tell him I want him out here within the hour." He dropped to the side of the bed and began pulling on his socks. "Oh and, Raz, don't mention this to Gracie or Lee. Okay?"

"Sure thing, Boss." The foreman nodded. "There's one other thing. Lefty saw some fresh tire tracks up by Leland's Ridge late yesterday."

Ralt stood. "Anybody been up that way lately with the jeep?"

"Not that I know of. Since that last flash flood, when we lost the bridge, it's been easier to go by horseback. It's nearly fifteen miles around Turndown Point if you drive."

A thoughtful gleam appeared in Ralt's eyes as he slipped into a fresh shirt, then tucked the tail into his jeans. "That means whoever is availing themselves of that part of our property is coming in by the creek, doesn't it?"

"Looks that way to me," Raz agreed. "Want me to get some of the boys and ride over there?"

"I sure as hell don't," Ralt snapped, then immediately clapped the older man on the shoulder. "Sorry, Raz. I didn't mean to bark at you."

"Don't apologize, son. I'm not in a much better mood myself. I think a lot of Gracie, and I like Lee. It

172

galls hell out of me to think of some son of a bitch threatening them."

"Well," Ralt rubbed at his chin, "Lee will be leaving shortly after lunch. Don't you think it's about time Gracie visited her sister in Baton Rouge?"

Raz nodded. "Sure do, boss. Sure do. Matter of fact, I'll go and tell her myself."

Later in the day, as Lee closed the last piece of her luggage, her eyes collided with Ralt's. He was sitting on the other side of the bed, watching her every move like a hawk. They'd said their good-byes last night and again during the morning.

"It's . . . been nice," she said softly, a tremulous smile breaking the smoothness of her face. It's been pure heaven, she would rather have said. "I don't think I'll ever see an orange sunset again without remembering this place."

"That coming from a city gal who swore she hated the country life?" Ralt smiled gently.

"Oh well." She shrugged, forcing down the huge lump in her throat. "Sometimes we don't know what we like till we try it, do we?"

The ambiguous remark wasn't wasted on Ralt. Tenderness softened the hardened features of his rough face. "No, honey, we don't. And just as often, we find that what we really do want is the worst possible thing for us."

"Why are we speaking in riddles, Ralt?"

He considered several excuses. It wasn't easy being honest when that same honesty was going to deprive them of their happiness. Yet he owed Lee. In more ways than one. "I'm afraid for you," he said simply.

"Nonsense," she tried to sound brave. "More likely you're as big a coward as I am." For some reason at that particular moment she felt brave . . . reckless. "The only thing we're afraid of is the future."

"Maybe so, Ms. Cantrell." He smiled. "But I want to know that you're safely back in New Orleans by this evening." He explained about the note found earlier.

"Oh, God, that's frightening."

"Don't you worry, we'll take care of things. It's just important that you leave as soon as possible; we're also sending Gracie to visit her sister. It will be much easier getting to the bottom of this without having to worry about the two of you."

She nodded gravely. "I'll miss you, cowboy." Her voice was barely audible and moisture in her eyes blurred his image. She hated the creep responsible for ruining these last few moments. "Let me know what you think of my article. Okay?"

Ralt rolled to his feet, flexing his hands as he prepared himself to leave her. "I'll do that, kid." He looked over his shoulder at her. "Next time you go horseback riding, think of me. Okay?"

"I'll do that . . . McLean."

The moon slid behind a cloud, casting the rocky slope into inky darkness. Ralt felt a sharp rock biting into his side. He eased to the left a few inches, cursing profusely at whatever fates that saw fit to put him on the hard ground behind some damned rock in the middle of the night as he attempted to catch the cattle thieves in the process of purloining half his herd.

"Having problems, Boss?" Raz chuckled as the

174

curse words fell around him. They were on the precipice overlooking a valley where a large herd of cattle had settled for the night.

"Hell, yes," Ralt snapped in a near whisper. "I'm having several problems trying to figure out why some damned ass has decided to reduce my herd just because I have more cattle than he thinks I should."

"Put like that, Raz, he has a point," the sheriff, Clive Ramsey, answered with gruff amusement.

"How nice of you to agree," Ralt said sarcastically. "However, what with losing nearly fifty head within the last week, I don't give a damn whether anyone agrees with me or not."

Suddenly all three men heard the distinct sound of a vehicle. Clive Ramsey gave quiet orders to several other deputies positioned at strategic points. The reappearing moon showed the guns each man carried, and revealed the seriousness of the situation.

"Ready, Ralt . . . Raz?" Clive asked.

"Ready."

From around a curve, twin beams of light came into view. The powerful engine of an eighteen wheeler lent its throbbing cadence to the surroundings. When the engine was cut, there was silence. The deputies spread out, darting and dipping behind outcroppings of rock till the truck was surrounded.

When the doors opened and a man stepped down on either side, the quiet was shattered with several warning shots, raised voices, and utter disbelief for the culprits.

* * *

Cole read the last sentence, closed the magazine, then looked at Lee, his expression unreadable. They were in his office, and Lee was anxiously awaiting his reaction.

"Well?" Lee prodded him. "What do you think? Is it okay? Was I thorough enough?"

"I said it before I gave the final okay to print and I'll say it again: It's a damned fine piece of work, Lee."

"Really, Cole?" she asked suspiciously. It had taken her two weeks and no telling how many crumpled, discarded pages before she'd come up with the final draft. To her, it was the most important piece of work she would ever do, and it was imperative that it be perfect.

"Really." He grinned. "You've presented a Ralt Mc-Lean that comes over as very human, one never before seen by the public. I'm impressed. You really got to know the man, didn't you?"

Lee ducked her head, her face a mask of conflicting emotions. "Yes," she finally answered. "I got to know him exceptionally well."

"And?"

"And . . . nothing. He has his life, I have mine. You know the rest: and never the twain shall meet."

"I'm sorry, Lee."

"Don't be. Contrary to popular belief, McLean was honest with me. I could even go further and say he put my safety above everything else."

"Then why aren't you happy? You've just accomplished the impossible." He indicated the magazine. "You've succeeded where so many others have failed."

176

"That's a good question, Cole. When I find the answer, I'll let you know."

She returned to her desk in time to answer the phone.

"How are you?"

Lee cocked her head to one side, a half smile on her face. "Lance?"

"In the flesh. How's it going, kiddo?"

"Great," she said promptly. "Are you in town for a game?"

"Shame on you," he chided her with suspect censure. "Kickoff's at seven o'clock at the superdome."

"Sorry, I must have overlooked it."

"Don't apologize. How about a late dinner after the game? It's been a while and I'd like to see you. Matter of fact, I have some news I'd like to share with you."

Lee's first impulse was to say no. But something kept her from doing so, some inexplicable thread that still controlled their relationship. "Sounds nice." After deciding on a time and place, Lee replaced the receiver, almost ready to kick herself for opening old wounds. Yet, she reasoned, her life with Lance was something she was going to have to come to terms with. She couldn't allow it to haunt her forever . . . and Lance would be the first to point that out.

The remainder of the day was spent with one eye on the clock till quitting time. The first thing Lee saw as she rounded the corner of the corridor where her apartment was located, was two men in gray delivery uniforms. As Lee got closer, she saw that they had a washing machine set on one dolly and a dryer on another.

177

"Ms. Lee Cantrell?" the shorter of the men asked.

She nodded. "Yes. What can I do for you?"

"Show us where you want these babies put."

"I beg your pardon?"

"It's right here, lady," the other man spoke up. He indicated the clip board resting on top of the washer. Lee walked over and looked at the order. Sure enough, there was her name, big as day.

"But I didn't buy these," she continued to protest. "There has to be some mistake."

"No mistake, lady." Short-stuff shook his bald head. "The order came in this morning. We were told that if we didn't make delivery, we'd lose our jobs. Surely you don't want that to happen, do you?"

Approximately forty minutes later, Lee stood back and surveyed the new almond-colored appliances. Apparently Messrs. Lowe and Hunter had finally opted to do the right thing, she decided. She ran a hand over the shiny surface. Nice. It would be a relief to do her washing and not have half of it disappear.

At seven o'clock Lee was settled in front of the television, watching the duel between the Wingers and the Commodores. It turned out to be one of Lance's most successful games. As she saw how easily he was able to throw the passes and even run for yardage himself, Lee knew he still had a number of years left to play. That pleased her. His game meant more than anything else in the world to Lance.

When he picked her up later, he was all smiles. There was a red abrasion on his chin, a scratch on his right cheek, and a bruise underneath his right eye.

"Well," she mused as she stood back and stared at

178

him, her arms crossed over her breasts. "You look like an overgrown boy who's been in a neighborhood brawl." She stepped forward then and kissed him on the cheek. "Congratulations on the game." From then until they arrived at the restaurant, the talk was football.

All during the conversation, Lee found herself amazed at how comfortable she felt with Lance. Yes, she told herself, the word was still "comfortable"—not at all exciting. It was as if he were an old friend in town for the night.

They were halfway through their meal, when Lance looked hard and long at her. "Is there a spot on my nose?" she asked laughingly.

Her soft chuckle was heard by a tall, dark-haired man dressed in a conservative gray business suit. He was seated with two men at a table a few feet away. He quickly turned in his chair and looked behind him, his blue eyes icy, his body almost visibly recoiling as he saw Lee and recognized the man she was with.

"No spot," Lance said quietly. He looked into his wineglass, then back at Lee. "I'm engaged."

For what seemed like an eternity, Lee sat unmoving. Had she heard correctly? The thoughts in her mind reminded her fleetingly of a huge rummage sale. That's right, a rummage sale. Nothing matched and nothing was in its rightful place.

This was her Lance. She wasn't ready to cut that final tie with him, even though she knew she didn't love him anymore.

"Are you sure?"

"Sure?" He considered her for several assessing seconds. "Reasonably so. There isn't the magic we had, Lee. I don't ever expect to have anything like that again. But I really think I love her. Are you going to be happy for me?" An inward sigh tore at Lance. He'd have given anything in the world if it had worked between them. She would always be special to him . . . always. He reached for her slender hand and held it in his warm grasp, understanding in his eyes. "Let it go, honey. I've wrestled with it ever since we parted, and couldn't change a single solitary thing. It's hell losing a good friend and getting a divorce at the same time."

Their gazes met and held. Pictures of the past marched with swift precision through their minds, pictures that would be with them always but would no longer dominate any part of their lives.

"Be happy, Lance," Lee finally managed, and immediately felt a soft, gentle lifting of a weight from her shoulders. She raised her wineglass in a toast. "To the future."

Lance sensed her release on the past and smiled. He raised his glass. "To the future."

As if propelled by fate, the man in the gray suit chose that moment to again turn and observe the couple. He saw the salute, the happy smiles on their faces and felt a swift pain in his gut.

Damn her! Damn them both!

After that initial burst of fury, however, common sense took over. He turned back to his dinner companions, ignoring their open curiosity. He wasn't the least concerned with what they thought of him. They wanted his money. He wanted the green-eyed beauty seated behind him.

"Well, Ralt," the eldest of the two men spoke. "Do you like what you've heard so far?"

"I believe it has possibilities, Ira. Definite possibilities." He surprised them by pushing back his chair and standing. There was no way in hell he could sit by and let another man walk off with the woman he loved. One hand slipped inside his jacket and came out with a business card. "Call me in three days. In the meantime, have a copy of the prospectus delivered to my office." He shook hands with each man. "I'm sure we'll be doing business together, gentlemen. Good night."

The astonished duo watched him walk to the other table, say something to the tall, blond man and the pretty woman. They saw him pull out a chair and sit down. The man was curious, the woman shocked.

"Hello, Lee. You're out kind of late, aren't you?" Ralt asked. He extended his hand to Lance. "I'm Ralt McLean. I'm in love with Lee, and I intend to marry her."

The other man shook his hand. "Lance Porter. How does Lee feel about marrying you?"

"McLean has a unique habit of going about things backwards, Lance." Lee spoke for the first time. Her hands were trembling so badly she kept them tightly balled into fists in her lap. "He thinks all he has to do is deem it so and it will happen."

Ralt simply stared at her for several seconds, his eyes feasting on the sight of her. "Are you happy with your new washer and dryer?"

"You!"

"We 'high-powered' executives have our uses." He

181

grinned. "I also liked your article. First honest piece that's ever been written about me. It was also pointed out to me by Raz and Gracie that the person doing the writing cared deeply for me. Care to elaborate?"

"No," Lee whispered, unable to cap the excitement starting to build within her.

"Then will you marry me, Lee Cantrell?" Ralt knocked the socks off her by proposing. He was pulling the biggest bluff of his life. If it worked, he would be the happiest man on earth. If it didn't, then . . .

Lance looked expectantly from Lee to Ralt. What he saw was a fantastic thrust of feeling and love and desire pulsing between them. He studied this man who seemed to have finally won Lee's heart. Ralt McLean. Lance knew him only by reputation but he liked what he was seeing.

"Are you asking, McLean?" Lee countered.

"Yes, ma'am," he said innocently, biting at the corner of his lip to keep from laughing at her. At that precise moment he wanted nothing more than to reach across the table and pick her up into his arms. He wanted to feel her small, hot body against his . . . wanted the scent and taste of her permeating his senses.

Suddenly he couldn't stand the waiting any longer. He stood. "Have you and Lance finished here?"

Lee looked at her ex-husband and smiled as they pushed back their chairs and rose. "Yes. You could say that. I wish you all the happiness in the world."

"And you," he murmured, then bent down and brushed his lips against her cheek.

182

"Just do one last favor for me, Lance," Lee said quietly.

"Name it."

"Don't wait till you're a physical wreck before you retire."

"I'll think about that." He grinned. He turned to Ralt. "If Lee says yes, you'll be a very lucky man."

Ralt nodded. "I know that already, and she *will* say yes."

After that, Lee was never quite sure how the three of them parted nor what was said. The drive from the restaurant to her apartment was made in record time. Quiet record time. She was tongue-tied, and Ralt didn't appear to be in much better shape.

As soon as they walked into her living room, Lee started toward the kitchen on the pretext of making coffee.

"Damn the coffee," Ralt said roughly. He caught her in his arms, his mouth covering hers hungrily.

With each heartbeat, Lee felt her body unfolding. He was the sun, she the rosebud, awaiting the magic of his warmth to unfurl the silken folds of desire lying somnolent within her. Firm hands made long, whispering sweeps over her body, slipping inside the bodice of the yellow dress she was wearing and caressing her full breasts.

Lee was aching from wanting him. Spirals of desire were setting off rivers of need, urging her closer and closer to the source from which her relief would come. Her arms crept up to his neck, her mouth eagerly responding to his commanding one.

"Oh God!" Ralt shuddered, dragging his lips across

hers to the softness of her neck. "You're in as bad a shape as I am, aren't you?" At her feeble nod, he went on. "I can't stand another separation, Lee. Marry me, live with me . . . I don't care which. Let's just not torment each other again."

"Love me, McLean," she whispered.

"Oh yes, sweetheart. It will be my pleasure."

He picked her up and carried her to the bedroom. "The door on the right or the left?" he asked as he entered the hall.

"Right," Lee said dreamily. This was heaven and she would kill anyone who told her differently. When Ralt set her on her feet beside the bed, he cupped her face with his hands.

"First things first, Lee Cantrell," he said gruffly. "I love you. I've never loved another woman. You're the first, and you'll be the last."

"That's heavy, cowboy," she answered shyly. "But in case you're searching for like to like, then you can stop looking. I'm not sure what to call my feelings for you. All I know is, when I left Texas, I left my heart."

Ralt bent and touched his lips to hers, a crooked grin touching his sensuous lips. "I'll make do with that till something better comes along. In the meantime, Ms. Cantrell, darling, I plan on making love to you all night long."

"Why, Mr. McLean," she replied demurely, "you have such a charming way with words."

They fell in a heap on the bed, hands and mouths hungry for each other. Ralt touched and stroked and caressed till Lee was writhing in precious agony, calling his name with the breathlessness of a lover. And he was her lover, he thought gratefully . . . now and for always.

He took a rosy nipple between his lips and teased it with his tongue, then immediately paid the same delicate attention to the other one. From there he kissed his way to the hidden secret of her navel. He laved the tiny recess lovingly, then moved lower, to the silken refuge awaiting his attention. With each flicking foray of his tongue, he felt Lee's trembling response.

When her fingers became lost in his hair and pulled him back over the same raging path he'd opened, Ralt settled in place over her, his legs slipping between her honey-colored thighs. He pressed his manhood against her, but before he made the final plunge, he caught her chin in one hand and forced her to look at him.

"I've changed my mind," he said. "I do care whether or not you live with me or marry me. I won't settle for anything but marriage. Understand?"

"Of course, McLean," she sighed dreamily, her eyes luminous emerald pools. "Anything you say."

He entered her then, and took Lee's breath away. The crescendo of passion was nesting, growing, then burgeoning into an explosive eruption. On and on it went till time and surroundings became indistinguishable.

Ralt was with her. She was with Ralt. They were together.

They soared . . . they dipped, then soared again.

The climactic moment burst upon them, flung them into the realm that only lovers know, then slowly brought them back to reality.

* * *

Lee gently rubbed her chin against the broad chest, the wiry hair tickling her. Something wonderful had occurred between her and Ralt. Something that had been missing during the previous times they'd made love.

"Is that a sigh of contentment or longing?" Ralt asked. One hand rested on her back, the other behind his head.

"Contentment, cowboy, contentment. You're a very nice lover."

"That's good, considering I'll be your lover for the rest of your life."

Lee pushed herself into a sitting position, dragging the spread with her. "What made you change your mind, McLean?"

"Loneliness," he answered with hesitation. "After you came back to New Orleans, it was all I could do not to come get you. Your presence was everywhere. I think I've loved you since that day when you came storming out of nowhere and interrupted my hunting."

"You've conquered your fear that I'll come to harm?"

"I think I've put it in its proper perspective," he corrected. "I'll always worry. But I'll beef up security and stop looking for a spook behind every tree."

He watched her for several seconds. "What about you? You seem to have had a great change of heart. Care to elaborate?"

"I buried my ghosts this evening. Lance is engaged to be married." She frowned. "Somewhere in all the confusion, I think I've been feeling guilty. I couldn't make the marriage work, I made Lance miserable, and I lost my best friend."

"And now?"

"He's happy. That's the reason I went out with him this evening. He wanted to share his news with me."

"I don't mind telling you, I was scared as hell when I discovered you sitting there with him. I was convinced you were about to elope. That was the impetus I needed to bring my thoughts together. The two men I was having dinner with must have thought I'm crazy."

"Oh, Ralt." Then her eyes darkened. "What's been happening with the rustlers and the committee dealing with the illegal aliens?"

"The rustlers have been caught, including the accomplice working on the ranch who took care of the note. He was one of the new hands Raz hired when the rustling first started. Convenient, hey?"

"And how." Lee chuckled. "Was it a real shoot-'em-up-type capture?"

"Shotguns and all." He grinned. "Seriously, no one was hurt, and it's over . . . at least for a while. As for the alien situation, we're working hard. I don't know how successful we'll be, but I suppose each little bit helps."

"I'll be glad when you get off the committee. It frightens me," Lee told him. "By the way, I have a brother you haven't met. He's a pain, but he has a lovely wife."

"Why not ask them out to dinner tomorrow evening?"

"I'll do that."

"Anyone else?"

"Oh yes, there's Maria. She's my best friend. You'll see her in the morning. We always have coffee together on Saturday mornings."

"Do you want a big wedding or a small one?" Ralt asked curiously.

Personally, he wanted something quick and simple. But if Lee told him to hang from a limb and grin like a gorilla, he'd be up the tree in seconds.

"Very simple." She looked down at her hands, then back at Ralt. "Would you like to have the ceremony at the ranch?"

He remained perfectly still, contentment rushing over him. "I'd like that very much.

"Now," he said silkily, "we have several hours yet before daylight. Do you have any idea how we can spend those precious hours?"

Lee pretended to ponder the problem. "Of course we don't want to do something as mundane as sleep, do we?"

"Indeed not."

"Eating in bed is tacky."

"My sentiments exactly."

"We can always read."

"We can always exercise."

"How innovative."

"Like that idea, mmm?"

"Oh yes. I especially like the way you're massaging my shoulders and my back and my . . . er . . ."

"Yes, my darling?"

"Mmm."

"What did you say, dear?"

"Oh, McLean . . . Ooooh!"

"You were saying, precious?"